C000095581

Prisms

By Amy Durrant

To Matt.

Best wishes, I hope you
enjoy the book!

Take Care,

Amy Durrant

Rainstorm Press

Rainstorm Press
PO BOX 391038
Anza, Ca 92539
www.RainstormPress.com

ISBN 10 – 1-937758-11-7
ISBN 13 – 978-1-937758-11-0

Library of Congress Control Number: 2012944170

Prisms
Publisher: Rainstorm Press
Copyright © 2012 by Rainstorm Press
Text Copyright © 2012 Amy Durrant
The moral right of the author has been asserted.
All rights reserved.

Interior book design by –
The Mad Formatter
www.TheMadFormatter.com

Cover Design by: © Amy Durrant

For Mary and Grace

Prologue

Frost danced across the blackened windows of Tine Street as Faye felt the wind whip past her flushed face. All seemed quiet and all looked still, but she knew things were not always as they seemed.

She knew all her focus was needed if she was to succeed, so she dropped even lower to the ground as she raced through the night, avoiding the streetlamps.

The shops she passed were barely visible in the low light and many of the names unfamiliar to her. Many, just empty shells and dusty shelves; a stark comparison to before the Runners.

Faye stopped, her breath hung in the cold night air as if suspended in front of her. "The Runners can't touch you," Faye reassured herself. "The Runners don't even know you exist."

Of this, she was sure. They knew about David in London, Lark in Hem and Clare caught between both worlds, but as of yet, they did not know her.

This was the first time Faye had allowed herself to gather her surroundings. Knowing the danger of her being in Centar, Faye climbed part way up the stone wall and crawled behind the shop sign above the doorway.

As her eyes adjusted to the unfamiliar darkness, she fiddled with the patch on her neck and reminded herself again of why she was here. But as she tried to find the reminder, she was distracted by the pattern of the street cobbles and a rusting blue chair outside 'Simms and Sons' opposite.

She knew this place, and not only did she know it, she remembered twirling a lock of topaz hair between her fingers and swinging her legs on the cobalt chair. Faye grew up in this very street and had once run up and down the silver cobbles for very different reasons to the ones she was forced to run for now.

The silence was broken by screaming from just up the street. Faye's gaze snapped to her right, just in time to see the flash of light that ended the tortured noise.

The air again turned still. This was wrong. Faye understood that silence meant danger and there was no need for the Runners to be out tonight. No one could out run the Runners.

Faye knew at this point she had three options. She could face them and lose, or disappear. Normally Faye would just disappear, but not tonight. Tonight was different and she would have to reach him no matter what.

One brief moment of pain and Faye's plan may even succeed. Choosing the third option and repeating in her mind "It's just a plaster, it's JUST a damn plaster," Faye reached for the patch on her neck.

In one swift movement the patch was gone, to be replaced by Faye's own screaming. Spasms of pain shot through her, her eyes flaming red as the torture continued.

Waiting for the pain to stop and sensing the Runners gaining speed, Faye finally felt herself changing. The adrenaline kicked up from her legs with such force she was thrown to the ground below.

And so, she began her race to find him, before the Runners found her.

Chapter 1
Anna Link

"FAYE!" Plates crashed against a metallic surface and the sound of a radio being retuned could be heard throughout the house. Faye tried to ignore the static and flipped the page of her book with more vigor than normal to highlight her annoyance. Surely it wasn't time for dinner already? She'd only been reading for what felt like an hour.

Glancing over at the alarm clock on her bedside, Faye noted that she'd been stuck into the book for at least four hours. Probably time to admit defeat and retrieve the bookmark that had been hastily cast aside amid all the excitement.

It wasn't often that she got some time to herself. If it wasn't mum needing a hand not burning food, then it was the decrepit next door neighbor who'd lost their cat up a tree. Again.

Tap, tap, tap on the window downstairs. Dax must be back, he was the only one who was stupid enough not to use the doorbell.

"Faye, door!" Faye heard her mum quite clearly, but was ignoring her by choice. Pretending not to hear was a much more successful method of dealing with her mother than returning the call.

Faye hated her proper name, Anna Link. It was a cross between two worlds and both worlds made sure she never forgot that. In London, her friends affectionately called her a hybrid and in Centar ... Well, the few friends she did have called her an experiment. What a lovely bunch of upstanding young adults, Faye mused to herself.

Faye heard more clattering from the kitchen downstairs and the sound of a door clicking open and being slammed shut against the battered framework.

Faye had pretty much exhausted all options for entertainment in her room. After all, there's only so much you can do when you've read what feels like a libraries worth of books and non-fiction essays.

"Mum, I'm home!" a male voice hollered from downstairs.

Sometimes, Faye felt a bit sorry for her mum. It must be hard being a practically single mother with a nineteen year old son who was just about as demanding as a three year old drama school child.

Flipping her topaz hair out of her eyes, Faye stretched out along the length of her bed and tried to burrow deep into the wealth of pillows at her headboard. But no matter how hard she tried, she just couldn't burrow deep enough to escape the impending train wreck that was family dinner night.

Both Faye's mother and father had separated when she was very young, so visiting two parents in different places was difficult at best. Although, the separation did have its advantages. At least she got two lots of ice cream instead of one and enough trips to the cinema to see all her favorite films.

Reaching round for the remote, Faye gave up her feeble escape attempt and began to channel flick. Someone had died on the news, a soap opera star had woken from a coma to find his wife sleeping with his best mate, some students were under arrest yet again. Nothing much was on, as is so often the case when you're not really looking for anything in particular.

Out of the corner of her eye, Faye caught a glimpse of the picture of her dad. He was beaming up at the camera from some sort of contraption designed for the waves. It might've been a speed boat, but it was impossible to tell underneath all the designer gear and dials.

She didn't really care what he did as a job. In fact, Faye didn't really care what he did at all. Her dad had been absent for so much of her life that he might as well have not bothered with the occasional Christmas card he sent if he remembered. Maybe that was where Dax got it from, Faye thought. It would make sense that a useless father would give birth to an equally useless son.

Speaking of the devil, Faye heard her brother banging around in the living room, searching for what she presumed to be the table mats. An almost impossible mission for someone so commonsensically challenged. It was a miracle that they were related, really. Dax was essentially the complete opposite to Faye.

Her brother and her counterpart, Dax liked risk where Faye liked comfort zones. Dax liked drinking Gin at three in the afternoon, whereas Faye liked to idle away the hours songwriting.

"Have you got the remote upstairs?" Dax hollered.

Again, Faye chose to ignore the cry. Having not bothered to come home for about a year, Faye didn't see why she had to talk to her brother, let alone surrender the remote to him.

"Dax, there's no point putting the TV on, we're about to have dinner!" Faye's mum retorted.

Why me? Faye asked herself. Why can't I be part of a conventional family who all live on the same world? She huffed and stood to glare out of the window. Tiny droplets of water formed on the pane and ran down, making it look like the fogged glass was misting up and crying.

"Dax, get out of the kitchen, go on! Go and get Faye," a now beyond irritated mother screeched.

It was inevitable, family dinner night could not be escaped. Faye sighed, went back to her bed and crossed her legs then buried her head deep within the pillows again. Without looking, she fumbled for the remote to her stereo and began playing the first track off the CD that was still lodged in there. David Bowie's classic Suffragette City blared out of the speakers accusingly and managed to muffle the last chink of cutlery that appeared to be steadily getting louder.

Tonight's topics for conversation would include: "Why haven't you got a job yet Faye?", "How's your father?" and then of course, "What do you mean you haven't spoken to your father?" It was the same, week in, week out. Naturally, Dax always managed to evade the barrage of questions ... somehow. Just as well really, considering that Dax worked the Maran black market. If mum ever found out that he sold illegal neck patches to holidayers trying to get through the Lamplight, Faye was fairly sure he'd be served up for dinner next.

Dax swung round the top of the banister and into the open doorway of Faye's bedroom. The wall of music hit him as he came in and saw that she was lying on her patchwork quilted duvet, legs crossed, head swallowed up by the bed. Faded posters of old bands cluttered the walls and the peeling daisy chain wallpaper was barely visible. There were no blinds or curtains on the windows, so that if Faye became homesick, her room was brightly lit by the sun or the stars and moon at night. Given her half-Maran heritage, she didn't like to stay in one place for too long if the colors were not vivid enough.

Ignoring Dax's arrival, Faye reasoned that it was a well-known fact that color played a large part in Maran life; mainly because the people who lived there looked like walking paint palettes. You may pass a woman whose eyes were deep purple with streaked orange hair or a man with emerald irises and locks the color of chocolate. In comparison to her mother, Faye's father was a sight to behold.

"Faye, can you turn the music down?" Dax tested, his voice just carrying over the chorus. "Faye, turn it down!" he shouted, his voice now audible over the ancient riffs.

"What!" A pair of smoldering crimson eyes glared up from under a curtain of topaz hair. Dax faltered for just a fraction of a second and decided it was safe enough to sit on the edge of the bed.

"What do you want Dax?" Faye snapped. "I've not got the remote."

Dax grinned and shrugged her question off.

"Where've you been for the last … forever?" There was real anger in her eyes as she spoke, reminiscing about the many times Dax had let her down in the past. Obviously it didn't matter to Dax if it was her birthday, or Christmas; or her nearing graduation. Even when Faye had learned to ride a bike for the first time, Dax had charged her for the lessons and left without so much as a goodbye.

In response, a number of emotions played across his face until he said, "I just thought I'd come and say hi."

Faye's eyes were like razors, so Dax decided against taking it any further.

"Yeah that was a joke. You know, something people laugh at? Dinner's ready," said Dax, as he punched Faye playfully on the arm.

"I thought you were something people laugh at," Faye jibed. She did not look impressed.

"Man you're up tight!" Dax offered in defense. "Ahh whatever. I'm guessing you're ignoring mum? She's called like ten million times."

"Like it's your problem," Faye spat. "You're never here. I'm surprised you remembered how to get home. If you can even call it that anymore," she added under her breath.

Dax considered this for a moment. "Excuse me, I have as much right to live here as you! Anyway, I've got a photographic memory." He winked and brushed his fringe out of his face.

Faye reached for the remote and paused the music. She spun round to face him and stood up, towering over him. "I ask you a serious question and you can't give me a straight answer!" Faye fumed.

Dax just smirked.

"For the love of Mara, it's like your mind filters through anything important and ignores it! We've not spoken in a year, Dax. You didn't even write to me. I mean, how hard is it to pick up a pen! I know you're used to other people doing things for you, but it's not that hard. At all," Faye accused, as tears began to well in her eyes. "Now you expect to waltz in here like nothing's happened and act like you're my brother again? You of all people know that's not how it works. You're exactly the same as dad."

As Faye tried unsuccessfully to storm out of her bedroom, Dax fought against her flailing arms to pull her into what looked like a hug. Really it was more an act of restraint.

"I'll come at you like a buzzard, I'm warning you!" Faye screamed. "Don't test me Dax."

Dax simply stood waiting for the calm after the storm and laughed lightly before whispering in a completely serious tone. "Are you quite finished?"

Faye glared up at him and ground her teeth together.

He sighed and continued, "Okay, okay, look I couldn't come back. I had no choice. I was really caught up at work and it was hard to get back ..."

Dax hadn't finished his sentence before Faye cut in. "Ahh that's fine then. You said it's all okay, so it's all okay. Phew, thanks for clearing that up for me, good job!" She flipped Dax a thumbs up before breaking out of his hold and began her descent toward dinner.

"Faye, c'mon just listen for a sec! I genuinely had to stay away for reasons ... I mean, I can't really explain them ... but you've got to believe me when I tell you it was out of my hands. I mean, it wasn't my fault!"

Faye stopped half way down the stairs and turned to face her anticipating brother. "Yeah, you know that 'believing you' thing?"

she said bitterly. "I'm kind of having trouble with that at the moment." The steps creaked ominously as she stomped down to face her mother.

"Faye just listen to me. I guess I'm…" Dax paused, as if having trouble finding what to say. There was rising urgency in his voice as he tried to find the words that would make her stop. "I guess I'm sorry … for missing everything and stuff … but you're gonna have to bear with me for this next bit."

It worked. Faye halted and began to twist the silver ring on her right finger as she fought back annoyance and anger. She spun one last time to look into her brothers eyes and crossed her arms as she fell silent, waiting for his explanation.

"For want of a better way to phrase this, I'm fairly sure our family is in quite a bit of trouble. Without wanting to sound too dramatic … we're probably going to be in grave danger very soon."

Faye began to calm and laughed exasperatedly as she tilted her head to face her now sincere brother. Then she hissed, "Nice way of not sounding too dramatic. If this is your sick idea of a joke, then you're far more twisted than I could ever have imagined."

Dax squared his shoulders and nervously cleared his throat before he proceeded with his piece. "Yeah, maybe that wasn't the best way of going about that. But no, I may be twisted but I'm not kidding. The whole boy who cried wolf thing doesn't really work in my favor here, but I'm being serious. I'd never place our family in that situation … but I think dad might. I've got no reason to lie and I know you don't trust me but you've got to believe me."

Faye glanced down at her feet and shrugged. "There's too many 'buts' in that sentence for my liking. Sorry."

He took a breath and bit his bottom lip; taking in the smell of burnt sauce wafting up from the kitchen and family photos that lined the staircase wall one last time before he shattered Faye's world. "Faye, I think dad's the reason we're in danger."

Chapter 2
Dax Link

Around two hours had passed since Dax had confronted Faye with his news and she had insisted that they shouldn't talk within ear-shot of their mother. Of course, this was after telling him repeatedly that he should seek psychiatric help.

Their mother was paranoid enough already and nothing was worse than confronting an angry paranoid who'd just burnt the Bolognese. To pass the time, they'd watched reruns of an old TV series called F.R.I.E.N.D.S and had laughed along with the canned audience when necessary, so not to arouse suspicion. When they were sure that the Sponsors would be patrolling the streets and not the tube lines, Faye and Dax had left their house in Euston Square and jumped on the Circle Line to London Liverpool Street. Why was it even called the Circle Line anyway? The name was far too obvious, Dax thought. Obvious and outdated.

The train took a sharp turn and the fluorescent lights flicked twice, protesting the sudden violent movement. Dax watched as black walls blurred past and tiny sparks parted ways with the car-riage when the tube got too close. The tube lines had always con-fused him. He understood the general gist of the system but the interconnecting platforms and labyrinth of tunnels were not com-mon to find in Centar.

Centaran rail was notorious for its heavy handed pickpockets, but only took five minutes to reach the furthest towns in the coun-try. Trying to get anywhere fast in London was like challenging paint to dry quicker. Or rather, Dax imagined that was a fitting

13

simile.

All this crossed Dax's mind as he thought about where he was and where he could be. Given the choice, he would rather be in Hem with his fiancé, Kash.

Another sharp bend and what looked like an abandoned station whizzing past.

He had always placed such trust in his dad, but now he wasn't so sure. Dax smoothed a strand of his deep red hair out of his face and turned his copper eyes to face Faye opposite. She was sat quite still, staring out the window into the dark abyss and absent-mindedly chewing on her bottom lip.

An intercom crackled into life and the tube speakers sounded like they were trying to regain their former glory. The result was much less impressive than the speakers had probably first hoped for though and the sound of static just fizzled away in the background. It was annoying, so Dax tried to turn his thoughts to something else. But trying to change his train of thought just made him think more about the Sponsors so Dax shuddered, shifting nervously in the thread bare tube chairs.

Sponsors were fearful people during the day, but even worse at night. Their sole purpose was to ensure no one passed between worlds illegally and there were very few streetlamps left that were unmonitored. Dax guessed you could think of them as police officers on steroids; who would rather hack your head off with a hatchet than arrest you.

Faye was terrified. Dax could see it in the creases of her fore-head and in the way she wrung her hands together. The black hood shielded much of her face, but as they sat together on the train, Dax tried to remember he was a brother before a messenger.

"I love what they've done with the décor ..." he mumbled sarcastically, before he was cut short by Faye who glared at him from across the old tube carriage.

"We'll talk when we get there," she said, her voice full of venom. "If you've not got anything helpful to say, can I give you a piece of advice? Don't say anything."

Faye didn't hate her brother, not really. She just lost patience with him and his sense of humor very quickly. Dax just reasoned that his sense of humor was far higher than Faye's, so it was okay if she didn't understand his intellect.

Prisms

The train slowed as they pulled out of the dark tunnel and onto the dimly lit platform. Restricted travel after hours meant Liverpool Street was deserted, so they had the station to themselves. The carriage doors slid open sluggishly and Faye jumped lightly onto the platform. Dax followed behind the worn yellowing line of the platform edge and was fascinated by the old advertisements plastered along the walls. Faces of band members that no one remembered smiled at him as he passed. One poster even claimed that the new fragrance 'Betrayal' would make him irresistible. Dax had tried all manner of fragrances, then realized the reason none of them worked was because he was perfect just as he was. He never learnt that arrogance is not always a virtue.

An old vending kiosk that looked like it had been in disrepair for many years collected dust on the corner of the platform, old cigarette cartons piled behind the thin wire mesh. Dax climbed the worn steps and jumped the ticket barriers. Tickets were a dying phenomenon and in year DC12, it became apparent that there was little need for station guards in a place that was rarely used. It was a shame really when you thought about it, Dax mused. About a hundred years ago in the year 2012, the stations had been bustling with hordes of tourists eager to catch a glimpse of the Olympics. Now look at the station; crumbling and abandoned. It was a damn shame.

The screen on the other side of the barrier showed worldly leaders Jonathon Caine and Torre Fynn smiling as they talked across a long ebony table in conference, but the screen jumped and repeated the same loop of footage over and over. Several windows in the station had been smashed and graffiti scrawled across the wall reading, "Sponsor the state, not the students."

The students had been worst affected by the new sponsorship program and many congregated in pubs, forming secret societies of rebellion. It seemed the student thing to do really. If it wasn't socialists trying to turn any open-minded uni student, then it was one of the many rebellion groups trying to recruit potential activists. Damn their persuasiveness, Dax cursed.

Faye grabbed Dax's arm. "We've not got time to admire the art work idiot."

Dax turned back to his sister, holding his hands up in a motion of surrender and followed in her step as she headed to the back wall of chairs. Surprisingly, there was no rubbish cluttering the station.

All that was missing was a passing dust ball and it could've easily been a ghost town from a scene in an old western.

The save the planet scheme was cranked up a notch when the people of Earth realized they now had two planets to save. Newspapers were counted as unnecessary waste and the first law introduced by the conference disbanded all newspaper groups. Even The Sun and Murdoch's empire of glossy mags and tabloids were not safe. The news, it was decided, would be delivered through controlled websites and websites alone. There went all the decent news stories, mused Dax.

A browning leaf crunched under Dax's foot, making a horrible reverberating sound around the station. True, crime rates were at an astronomical low but when some poor soul attempted theft, or worse still assault, they were removed to stop it from happening again.

Dax shuddered as he thought about the process of removal, but concentrated his mind back on the task in hand. He dropped down next to Faye on an old metal bench and pulled back the hood that cast shadows across her face. Some might say she was classically beautiful, then add the words, "If she wasn't a hybrid." Her half Maran heritage often meant Faye found it difficult to settle among people, so found it easier to constantly switch between the two worlds. At least, that's what Dax thought. He'd never really been good at reading his sister or working out why she did the things she did. It reminded him of their tortured family holidays. They'd always been hard work and he'd always fallen out with sister. It was just the way things went.

* * *

5 Years Earlier.

"Faye, don't disappear. Can we at least check in with the French woman first, please?"

Dax glanced at his mother who was becoming increasingly agitated and wished that he could be somewhere else. Dad never came along on any of these so called 'family excursions'. What a constant let down.

"FAYE!"

Faye often ran off in search of photos to take or songs to write, because apparently the inspiration had carried her along and she couldn't stop. It was stupid really, Dax thought.

"Oi, half-breed!" Dax teased, shouting after his thirteen year old sister. He just caught a glimpse of her topaz hair disappearing round the corner before she was gone. Up an old street in Carcassonne, nowhere to be seen again.

"Dax, ask your sister to come back please! I can't find the woman. Why don't they have doorbells!"

The sun was at its highest point in the day and beads of sweat began to mat in Dax's fringe.

The flight over had been hard work and as per usual, he'd been sat in front of a screaming child. Hard work when Faye also happened to be a nervous flyer and insisted on crushing his arm with her deceptively strong hands. Why was it so often the case with women?

"Faye! C'mon, mum's going ape! I think the heat's getting to her brain," Dax hollered, completely forgetting that the breeze carried his voice and amplified it tenfold.

"Dax Tiberius Link, if you do not bring your sister back right now, I am not giving you ANY holiday money." Now that was a decent enough incentive for him to find Faye.

It was mid-way through August and leaves were already beginning to fall and twist from the trees, tinting ever so brown in the burning sun. Paintwork was peeling off the tired buildings and shutters that once were whole, were now slats of wood hanging from cracked windows.

Dax sauntered up the cobbled street after his sister and left his mother trying to figure out whether the entrance to the owner's Chateau really was up a grand balustrade staircase. He thought it probably wasn't, but that is was best not to say anything, just in case.

Turning the corner, he spotted Faye crouching over by an old stone wall, apparently cupping something in her hands.

"Faye, what are you doing? We're meant to be finding our villa, not acting like lunatics," Dax accused.

The church bell tolled two in the afternoon and its ominous chimes echoed through the street.

"Come look at this, it's beautiful," Faye said, as she beckoned for her less than interested brother to come over.

Ambling over to his sister, Dax crouched down and sighed. "It's just lizard, Faye. Is that what you're staring at?"

"It's amazing. It's so small but it's beautiful. In such a quiet village, even the geckos are chilled out. Look, do you want to hold it?"

"Why would I want to hold a lizard!? It's just a lizard, Faye, don't you care 'bout our holiday at all? We've only just got here and you'd rather be somewhere else, doing something else!" Dax said feeling exasperated and fed up by the heat. "Just leave it, mum's calling. You're always pulling something like this."

Faye bit her bottom lip and lightly shook her head. "I just thought you'd be interested. I guess I was wrong. I thought you might actually care, but whatever."

"Why would I care about a lizard! There's probably thousands of them everywhere!" Dax shouted.

"If you don't care, why are you here then? If it's all the same, why didn't you go and stay with dad instead of ruining this holiday!" Their voices began to carry along with the echo of the chimes, and then was replaced with their loud bickering.

"I don't want to be here," Dax fumed. "I got told I had to be. I'd rather have space from you and mum to be honest and I'd rather spend my time with my mates. Ahh, you're SO annoying! Man I wish I wasn't here."

A tear began to well in the corner of Faye's eye and she put the gecko down on the dry ground. Turning sharply on her heel, she marched back down the street toward the large Chateau.
"Fine, go and run to mum. See if I care! You're just a child Faye, looking for attention. Next time you want to ruin our holiday by showing me a stupid lizard, don't bother!"

* * *

That had been the last family holiday Dax went on. The whole thing had turned out to be an unmitigated disaster and on reflection, Dax realized he'd behaved ridiculously. Like a petulant child who never gets his own way, when the reality is unbelievably the opposite. If only he could have been a better brother, he would. But it seemed like an almost impossible task and he'd given up long ago.

He removed one of his gloves and grasped Faye's hand. "You're freezing," Dax said, half asking half stating. "Giving you my gloves seems like the, umm, brotherly thing to do here."

As he began to remove the checkered gloves, Faye stopped him. "I like to feel the cold; it reminds me I'm human."

Dax had never really considered this, partially because he counted himself more Maran than Human. It had completely slipped his mind that Marans responded to temperature differently to Humans. If there was extreme heat, a Maran's body would immediately adjust to match the temperature. Seemed that on Earth, it didn't quite work in the same way.

Dax watched his breath catch in tiny white clouds around his face and glanced once around the deserted station before tucking his hands into his pockets for extra warmth. The cool of the bench beneath his legs calmed his nerves. The air was still. Silent.

"Did dad ever tell you what he does? I mean, like for his job?" Dax questioned. Faye looked up, a mixture of confusion and impatience apparent on her face.

"No. I don't really care to be honest," Faye retorted. "It's not my business. I never got the same sugar coated stories he told you before you went to bed. I didn't even get so much as a Cinderella. So no, I guess I don't care."

Dax turned slightly from his sister and slipped his hands out of his pockets to play with a pendant on his neck. It was about the size of a pen lid and shaped like a prism with a blueish, purplish band around the middle. Dax thumbed the smooth sides and felt for the edges where the prism took shape. Faye caught a glimpse of the pendant as it refracted the colors of the spectrum onto the tiled ground.

Before she could ask, Dax said, "Yeah, dad gave me this. I never really got what it's meant to do, to be honest, and it looks like something you'd pick up from Five-Pound-Land." Strands of hair fell across Dax's face and were quickly removed by hands that were now quivering with the cold. Damn weather. "Sure, dad could be crazy at the best of times but he said if ever I needed help, all I had to do was stand in the Lamplight and twist the pendant. He was pretty serious when he said it."

Faye looked puzzled as she tried to reason how the tiny prism Dax spun between his fingers could help him. Or anyone at all, for that matter.

"Yeah, crazy. I know. I think it's linked to dad's job and I know that he works for the conference, but that's about all I know," Dax informed his sister.

Faye turned her head away and whispered, "Well you've never known much, so no change there then."

Pretending not to hear the jibe, or choosing to ignore it, Dax continued, "Seems the men in our family aren't really good with the whole sharing thing. He's an executive though, which is damn high up the conference food chain. I guess this necklace thing is something you get with the job description."

Faye searched for a real link between what Dax had said and how that meant they were in danger, but could find none. Instead, she tried to maintain an uninterested expression and fight back the confusion lines that were creeping across her forehead. "So, what exactly does an executive do if they're so important? Surprised you've never said anything before if it's such a hot topic of conversation." Faye's eyes accused Dax as she said this, but he saw a glimmer of interest in the light of her iris that confirmed she wasn't being entirely serious.

"Faye my darling, I kiss and tell on a need to know basis," Dax dismissed.

Faye scoffed, rolling her eyes and turning up the collar of her hoodie against the chill.

Dax tentatively brushed the fringe out of Faye's eyes then leant casually back against the grey wall, feeling the ridges of broken tiles press into his back as he did so. He turned toward his sister and huffed before saying, "Executives are one step down from worldly leaders. You know, Torre and Caine."

"Yes I know that much!" Faye cut across sharply.

Dax took a deep breath and let her comment wash over him, trying to take the high road. How did people do it?! Ignore jibes and be the 'bigger person'. Before his mind wandered too far astray, Dax came back on topic. "Well, most of the time they're honorable, decent guys but the job title also means carrying out their dirty work. Kind of like Mafia henchmen I guess."

Faye considered this for a moment and then Dax continued. "Whatever, I thought it was a pretty good analogy. Perhaps Dad was ashamed; I know I would be. I bet the only thing that kept him going was knowing that everything dishonorable he did was for the benefit of us."

Prisms

While Faye took a moment for the information to sink in, Dax continued to twist the pendant between his fingers. Just as it began to spin, Faye stopped it with one hand and searched Dax's face for any sign he was lying. It was hard to tell in the lowlight but deciding eventually that her brother was telling the truth for once in his life, she asked, "Right. Assuming you are telling the truth, how does this place us in danger? We're not exactly members of the conference or activists in some crazy resistance group are we?"

Dax coughed nervously and scratched his chin before directing his gaze elsewhere with all the subtlety of a dead horse falling on a car.

"Are we?" Faye repeated, more deliberately this time.

Dax caught his sister's gaze again and quickly removed the pendant from his neck. Attempting to change the subject, he placed it in one of Faye's hands and cupped her other hand over it.

"No, no, no, it's ... it's hard to explain, I mean it was only once or twice with ... actually, never mind. Just shut up and listen!" Faye pursed her lips together to form a hard line but Dax continued regardless. "Last time I talked to dad, he said there'd been disappearances within the conference. I'm not normally a worrying kind of guy, but that was one week ago and he hasn't been home or rung me since. It's like he's dropped off the face of the Earth. And off the face of Mara," Dax said, his voice cracking in between sentences.

Faye picked up on the broken voice that crept through his normal bravado. "Well, can't you reach him through the wire? Or his mobile maybe?"

"Yeah, well I've tried." Dax looked down at his feet as he said this and scuffed them against the cool metal of the bench; his collected emotion faltering for just a fraction of a second.

Faye removed one of her hands from the pendant and tilted her brother's chin until his face was in line with hers. Worry lines creased in his forehead and it was clear the usual bravado was now gone for good. Sincere concern lit up his irises. It terrified Faye.

"What did he say?" Faye questioned, pronouncing each word separately.

Dax stared into his sister's eyes then replied in a grave tone, "Nothing. The line was dead."

Chapter 3
Lark Lyre

"Tell us where you meet!" The Sponsor delivered another blow into the stomach of the gasping man. Lark tasted the bitter salt of blood on his tongue and watched, bleary eyed as the ceiling began to swim.

"I've told you already," he said through gritted teeth, "I'd rather die than betray everything we've worked for."

He was sent sprawling across the desk by the force of the Sponsor's fist. A high pitched ringing in his ears began and marks were visible on his cheek where the butt of a gun had been viciously rammed.

"Fine," roared the Sponsor. "You don't want to talk? We have no need for tight lipped, cocky students like you. So long, sunshine."

He raised his gun and held it to the back of the man's head. Removing the safety catch, his finger twitched on the trigger.

This was it, Lark thought. What it really comes down to. It was a bit disappointing, really. No life flashing before your eyes like in the movies, no grand realization about where things went so wrong. Just pain. Well, and death of course.

A messenger burst into the room gasping for air. Now this was the kind of thing that happened in the movies.

"You can't kill him, don't shoot!" the messenger cried. He didn't look much older than twenty and his eyes were full of terror. Hunching over his knees and drawing in quick breaths, he managed to rasp, "Mr. Fynn has use of him."

Talk about just in the nick of time.

Prisms

As procedure went, this was most unusual. A worldly leader wanting the life of a resistant student spared? Lark saw the Sponsor falter for a moment, as he tried to reason why a man of such power would care about someone so insignificant. After several minutes of silence, the Sponsor raised his gun and spread both hands in an act of submission. Lark squared his jaw and watched the guard with suspicious eyes.

"Well, Mr. Lyre," proclaimed the Sponsor, "it seems you are free to go then. Sorry for the ... inconvenience." He smiled wryly and placed his gun on the marble topped table.

Lark began to move away and as he did this, one of the Sponsor's spread hands clenched into a tight fist. Reeling back from the force of the blow, Lark clutched his nose, cursing and trying to fight off the fire that was burning up though his cheek bones. Blood trickled down his mouth as he tried to re-orientate himself. It felt to him as if the world was spinning and he was ten feet in the air spinning in the opposite direction. He couldn't collapse. He couldn't show weakness to the guards.

Stumbling forward, grasping for anything he could use to steady himself on, the student caught hold of an outstretched arm; an arm that belonged to a designer suit and spotless pair of black shoes.

"Lark," the man remarked.

All those in the room snapped to attention and the smirking Sponsor straightened up to wipe the smile from his face.

"Lark Lyre; how extraordinary to meet you. You come from the town of Hem do you not? Just on the outskirts of Centar?"

Still recovering his ability to speak, Lark nodded. He knew this man; the man behind the terror, the man behind the deaths of the students and the leader of Mara. This man had caused him so much pain and now Lark was face to face with the man he had resisted. He contemplated spitting in his face, but fought back the urge with every inch of his battered body.

"Sponsor, you may leave," demanded the man. "This student is now my personal responsibility."

With one quick bow, the Sponsor began walking to the oak door and if his eyes had been daggers, Lark guessed he would be dead.

The suit turned his attention again toward Lark. His piercing jet black eyes surveyed the bloody and broken student carefully, then he raised one hand to his manicured silver beard. "I'm sure you're aware of who I am, but let me formally introduce myself." His voice was deep, calculated. It had the tone of a man who had practiced speaking to perfection all his life, yet never actually spoken to anyone before.

Taking one step back and outstretching an aging hand with a signet ring on one finger, he announced, "I am Torre Fynn. You may call me Fynn. I find I have need of your services, boy. You should clean up first, and then we'll have a little chat about how you can help the conference. I will not speak to a broken child."

Patronizing. Lark shouldn't have expected anything different from such a heartless man. It wasn't open enough for Lark to have a choice and it felt like a rhetorical question, but he still felt the obligation to nod in agreement and reluctantly shook Fynn's hand. After all, he was on their territory now.

"Excellent!" Fynn beamed. "I will send for one of the healers immediately." The leader raised one hand and a shaky middle aged woman entered the room. In real terms she had been middle aged for at least twenty years, but at her age who was counting?

"Take Lark. Make sure he's fixed and fetch him new clothes."

She simply bowed, trying not to make eye contact with the man and took Lark by the shoulder, leading him through the grand oak door. Lark was trying his best to pretend he hadn't heard the hidden malice in the man's voice, but a grimace crept across his face regardless.

When he thought Lark had left, Fynn sat in the large leather chair behind the marble desk. Lark glanced over his shoulder as the doors closed to see the leader clasping both hands in front of him and addressing one of the room guards. He said, "Contact Jonathon Caine. Have him ready the others and bring the new program with him." As the guard began to bow and the grand doors shut, he continued, "Tell Jonathon we may finally crush this nuisance."

* * *

Lark didn't like being out of his comfort zone and as comfort zones went, at the moment he felt like a whale out of water. He hit the wall with an open palm and immediately regretted it. Each finger felt brittle enough to snap off and his hand burned. All these secrets and violent visits in the night gave him a headache, and it had to stop. He didn't even understand what the people in the conference did.

Kash would often tell him: "If you get involved in the conference, I won't be the one to accept the box with your name on it."

Lark had never really understood this, until one of his friends had bluntly explained it meant he was likely to die. He wasn't afraid of death. It was a necessary evil. A part of living.

Kash had always been straight to the point with him. He loved his sister to bits but she could be very unnerving at times.

Lark planted both palms on the same wall he'd just attacked and tried to focus his mind on anything but the pain. When their father had been removed for murder, Kash and Lark both vowed to change their names. Lark changed his last name to Lyre and Kash changed hers to Trix. They hadn't spoken with each other for at least a year, but Kash had recently contacted her brother advising him to avoid the lamplight. Bang up job he'd done of that, Lark reminded himself. He was probably inside one of the Lamplight towers, if not worse.

In fact, Lark had absolutely no idea where he was. Men with eyes as dark as night had taken him from his house in Hem and placed a nylon bag over his head. Lark felt like he'd lost. When faced with a force stronger than him, Lark could not have hoped to triumph over brute strength. Sure, he was strong, but not as strong as a man who probably chews tacks for snacks and nails for breakfast.

Lark rolled up the cuffs of his shirt sleeves and kicked off his shoes. If he was going to be here a while, he might as well try to make himself comfortable. He scoffed at the idea. The room had bleached white walls and one small chair in the corner. An off white mattress sat in the middle of the room draped with a type of black satin that could pass for a sheet. He'd lost track of exactly how much time had passed since he'd met Fynn, but Lark figured it must have been at least two hours.

The single small square window in the far wall let in little light, making Lark very claustrophobic. He grabbed the chair and placed it underneath the window. When he stood on the chair, he was met with an incredible sight. For miles around, all that could be seen was brilliant white light surrounding geometric tower blocks; polished black tower blocks. Great.

There had been legends and tales of this place, the Lamplight towers. Buildings that appeared only in the limbo between Earth and Mara had been rumored, but never proven real. And now, he was most definitely inside one of them.

"Well done genius," Lark spoke aloud to himself. "You're stuck in a room with no door and a window that keeps getting smaller."

All the blood had been cleaned away from his face, and the healing cream had already begun to work wonders on his nose. There were fresh clothes hanging from a single coat hook on the wall, jet black of course. Lark thought that for a race so diverse in color, they were really unimaginative when it came to clothing.

Lark slipped into the black slacks and buttoned his shirt to the top. As he did this, the collar began to itch and rub against his neck. He put his hand up to find the source of irritation and felt something strange on the left of his neck. Something unnatural that hadn't been there before he'd entered the room. Beginning to panic but attempting to keep his cool, Lark tried to recall everything that had happened since he'd entered the tower. Frantically searching his memory, he couldn't find what he was looking for. Mind you, a lot had happened since he'd entered the Lamplight and he'd had a bag over his head for the majority of it.

But it was definitely there, just underneath his left ear; a definite mark. It felt as if it had been carved into him and was now acting like some sort of loose nerve.

Lark cursed the lack of mirrors in his cell and began to pace like a caged animal, kicking the wall occasionally. As he walked back and forth along an imaginary line in the room, he felt a strange sensation under his skin.

It was hard to describe and not at all painful, just a mild sort of rippling sensation. Like when the hairs on your arm stand on end but inside his arm instead. Caught off guard by this new feeling, Lark flexed the muscles in his back and stretched out the aches and tensions in his body.

Considering he had taken a large amount of damage only hours ago, Lark felt awesome. There was a new lease of life about him and the extra adrenaline didn't make Lark's head spin as it once might have done. Instead, for once in his life, Lark actually felt powerful.

Prisms

As he tried to place the moment this had all changed, there was a knock. Similar to someone knocking on wood but with a metallic sort of sound to it.

Lark's eyes searched the room for the source of the sound to no avail. Then, there came a voice.

"Lark, I need you to remove the covering from your neck."

Still scouring the room for the location of the mysterious voice, Lark once again ran his hand over the notch in his neck. "Go to hell," he shouted back.

He didn't understand how he could've missed it the first time, but there was a distinct lining sitting across his marked neck. A lining the reminded him of a plaster. He didn't need to wear a plaster, he was tougher than that. Fiddling for the edge of the covering, Lark tried in vain to remove it until finally he felt a small jagged section. Holding it between his thumb and forefinger, Lark tore the lining away.

The effect was instant and Lark crippled to the ground in burning agony. The rippling sensation he had felt underneath his skin turned into waves that caused his body to contort and convulse, twisting and throwing him in different directions. Fire flew up his arms and screams escaped from between his clenched jaws.

Lark threw his arms back in an attempt to shake the excruciating pain, only to make it worse. His head felt so full of pressure Lark thought he would collapse, but the shocks pulsating through his body stopped him.

Only when he felt he would rather die than endure another second of this torture, did his body allow him to pass out. As the pain subsided, so did the light. The last thing Lark saw was a pair of frightened faces framed by black hair, staring at him from above.

Chapter 4
Kash Trix

Kash very rarely traveled outside of Hem. She had little reason to when everything she needed was at home. But now, she began to feel her world crumbling. Lark was missing, Dax had gone AWOL and she'd managed to break the only cube they had.

"Why don't you work like a human computer!" she accused. "'I offer multidimensional interfaces to improve your interfacing experience'; what does that even mean?"

She hit the cube, perhaps hoping it would jerk back to life, but it just sat on her desk quite broken. It made a sort of whirring noise before falling silent for the last time. The news network broadcast on cubes across the country every night at 6.00pm so any major change could be broadcast to the nation. Other than that, she only used it for uploading videos to YouCube.

Kash flipped her sapphire hair, glaring at the broken piece of technology with emerald eyes. After deciding that staring at an inanimate object was probably pointless, Kash retreated to the sofa and lounged across it, one arm trailing down the side.

"I hate all the mass production factories. In both worlds!" Kash shouted. "Especially the ones which try unsuccessfully to make copies of computers, which work VERY well as it is thank you very much!"

She lay on the sofa for a few minutes, cursing and shouting into a cushion before she decided to get up and do something. She reasoned that since finding a replacement cube was probably not that important in the great scheme of things, she should try to focus on finding Lark or Dax, since both of them had mysteriously disappeared. But then again, people disappearing wasn't really that uncommon in a world where you could simply nip to a different world if you stood under the right streetlamp.

Kash sauntered over to the front door of the flat and cracked it slightly to gauge what the weather was like. A breeze caught her by surprise and whipped a stack of papers into a frenzy that had been strewn across her desk. There had been terrible electrical storms for three weeks straight and though she'd hate to admit it, the thunder really frightened her. It was also the beginning of the cold season. Not that it would make much difference to her, Kash didn't feel the cold, but she loved the patterns left behind by frost after a chilly night.

Checking her wrist clock, Kash decided she would have around two hours of daylight to wander through the streets, in search of clues to her loved ones whereabouts. 'Super Detective' wasn't really in her personality description, but then again, who writes those descriptions any ways?

A green cat ran past the door, hissing as it went and jumped down off the metal walkway, onto some unsuspecting Maran's roof. The clatter of metal dustbin lids could be heard from further down the street and Kash wondered if they made the same clattering sound on Earth if they were disturbed. Maybe they didn't even have them on Earth.

Kash's mind often jumped between subjects very quickly and she barely had an attention span. When it was called for, she could act in a serious manner and think logically, but it was much more fun to experience life spontaneously with no real direction.

But as annoying as Kash could be, she knew she inspired those around her and her boundless energy would bring hope to the most dire of situations. Her friends had often joked she was a yo-yo, up down, up down, all day long. Now, her friends were long gone. Barricaded in a fort somewhere, trying to ignore the conference and its plotting, but not Kash. Not while she still had breath in her body would she submit to the violent Sponsors and their evil regime. She wasn't afraid of dying. Besides, they had a stupid name.

Kash stepped out onto the metal grill outside the flat and took in the scenery. Two blocks away an old woman rocked in a wooden chair on her balcony, twisting pieces of thread between her frail fingers. Kash saw the lamplights flick as people passed between worlds, moving from one life to another.

The Lamplight had always fascinated her, even as a young girl. She'd longed to know what it felt like to travel by the light and wondered what it would feel like to glimpse the towers of the legends. She still had so many unanswered questions.

Why could experiments pass freely but she couldn't? Was it true that on earth, you could throw snowballs until your hands grew raw from the cold? And was there really a magical drink called 'Red Bull' that gave you wings?! She'd never had the chance to find these answers; until she'd met Dax.

* * *

1 Year Earlier.

"You look freezing," the young man remarked to the girl sat among the snow. It was late into the cold season and neon lights lined the frames of shop windows. Another human festival was approaching, so in Centar there was a novelty in selling little trees and wrapping books in paper to give to each other as gifts.

The girl looked up. She had piercing green eyes and her hair was colored deep blue. On inspecting the girl, the young man corrected that she was in fact a young woman, perhaps aged eighteen or so.

"Your hair," he said admiringly. "I've never seen anything so …" he struggled for a moment, then added, "blue."

The young woman smirked and patted the space next to her on the step. She was sat in the doorway of 'Simms and Sons', a trader in absolutely anything and everything. From the marvelous to the monstrous, Simms stocked it.

"I prefer it described as sapphire," she joked.

There was a real warmth about her, something the young man had not encountered in a while. She gazed at him with inquisitive eyes and he knew he had never fallen for someone quite like this before.

"And I'm not freezing," the young woman stated. "I don't feel the cold. But thanks for offering me your jacket anyway."

The young man looked down at his hand and the red tailored jacket it was clutching. He looked up, half embarrassed half flattered that she'd noticed.

"It matches your red hair," the young woman laughed.

He twisted a lock of it between his fingers. "Yeah call it crimson. And now I'm holding it anyway, I should probably go ahead and offer you my jacket."

He stretched out his hand and the young woman declined. Instead, she removed the jacket and placed it on the step. With one hand now free, she slipped hers inside his and intertwined their fingers.

"For future reference, if you want to talk to a stranger, don't offer them an item of clothing as an excuse." The young woman smiled lightly and the young man smiled back.

"I'm Kash," she said, shaking the hand she was holding.

The young man looked at the ground and laughed, crushing the snow between his free fingers. "Then it's my pleasure to meet you Kash. I'm Dax." He kissed her hand and lingered for a few moments so that their faces were inches from one another. Then he leant forward so that his mouth was in line with her ear, and whispered, "Now if you're done blushing, I wouldn't mind enjoying this fine weather we seem to be having." As he said this, his other hand formed a fist in the snow and with surprising speed he jumped from the step and turned to throw the snowball at Kash.

In between shrieking insults about his precision and how she didn't stand a chance, Kash knew she had found her match. It didn't take much thought for her to accept Dax's proposal a year later either.

He wasn't always the most romantic of types, he was far more immature than Kash had first thought and granted he was a year younger than her, but every moment with him was a rush. Whether it be a rush of emotion or rush of excitement, Dax was her soul mate. Or, he would have been if she believed soul mates existed.

* * *

And now she'd lost him!

She stormed down the steps from her flat onto street level, avoiding the second step from the bottom that had been broken for years and began walking toward the station. From there, she intended on catching the next rail to Centar and starting her search for Dax. Perhaps she could live for longer without Lark, but she really needed Dax. He was like her own personal lifeline, in her own little world.

There were few people out on the streets now and the last remainder disappeared into the streetlights she passed. Shop keepers swept the steps of their trade and last minute shoppers rushed to catch the final rail home. A man dashed past her, catching her arm as he went and hastily apologizing for doing so.

As Kash walked with her head down, she noticed her breath hung around her in thick white clouds. She kicked the artificial leaves as she walked, watching them spinning and twirling on the breeze. While she knew they had been engineered by the conference to mirror the seasons of Earth, she still thought the deep brown colored leaves were beautiful to look at.

The sun began to set, throwing shadows across the cobbled streets of Hem and dancing across dark rooftops. She checked her wrist clock again; only one and a half hours left of daylight. Kash thought about the scale of her task and how impossible her mission might've sounded to a stranger, but she didn't care. In a world of so many possibilities, Kash knew nothing was impossible. Besides, it was her stranger she needed to find.

Chapter 5
Faye

Faye slammed the phone down and angrily kicked the rusting telephone box. Running her hands through her hair, she stepped out into the street and took in the London air. She heard the sound of a car speeding past a few streets down and distant laughing, drifting from an upstairs window, but the rest was silent.

She had never known a place to be so quiet before. London at night was like a ghost town. The once bustling bars and restaurants of Covent Garden were now in darkness. The thriving community were all either asleep or too afraid to trade at night.

Faye thought it was a shame really. She remembered seeing the street artists and fire eaters as they wowed the hordes of tourists and youngsters.

Once, she'd seen a wizard in grand purple robes casting spells on passers-by. With a shiny ten pence piece in her hand, she'd skipped to the wizard and dropped it in his hat. She'd watched in fascination as he'd raised his magic wand and tapped her lightly on the nose. Her mother hadn't been impressed having to drag a giggling toddler around London for the remainder of the day. Of course, wizards and warlocks and the likes were long gone now.

Remembering this, she looked around the street and felt a longing for her younger years. No restrictions, no problems. No Sponsors.

Walking toward the main square, she skimmed her hand along a smooth metal railing that ran parallel to one of the walls. Light from the moon reflected off the shop windows, casting eerie shadows across the pavement. The cobbles underfoot threatened to trip and throw her forward, but Faye knew them too well to allow it.

Up ahead, she saw Dax stretched out along one of the steps. He looked so still, so peaceful, it would have been easy to mistake him for a statue. His crimson hair had fallen over his face, so Faye couldn't tell whether he was asleep or not. It wasn't often Dax was silent and it was a good idea to make the most of it when he was. Frustrating Dax, Faye added to herself. Temperamental Dax.

She didn't hate him, not really. She would try to be annoyed but then he would smile, take one of her hands and she'd forget why she'd been angry in the first place. If only he wasn't so useless! She reached Dax and sat on the step below him, next to his head.

He titled his face so that Faye could see his eyes. "Did you get through?"

Faye bit her lip and scuffed her shoe against the pavement below. "No," she replied. "I talked to a Maran operator, but as soon as I asked for the missing persons line, the call was disconnected. They're doing a great job of not arousing suspicions, idiots."

After the disappearances had started, it had become virtually impossible to track down missing people. It was like the conference didn't want them to be found. Faye had her own theory that they were behind it, but she didn't have proof to back it up.

"You're not off the hook, you know," Faye snapped. "I'm still furious."

Dax sat up slowly and Faye saw a sudden urgency in his copper colored eyes. The time was about 1.00 am. One hour had passed since they'd got on another train to Covent Garden, and they weren't keeping to the shadows as usual. Very lax for Dax, Faye thought.

Keeping his voice low, Dax said, "Very slowly, look to your left. There's a guy just to the side of the Lamplight, tell me what he's wearing."

"Stop messing around, I'm not in the mood," Faye said, turning in the direction he'd suggested. "Oooh there's a guy, is there? Come up with a better way of getting my attention, then try again."

Then Faye's face turned cold as her brain caught up with what Dax was saying. Scouring the dark more carefully for a figure, she saw a man at the end of the street. He stood half in the Lamplight so that his face looked almost menacing and his shadow cast along the length of the cobbles. Faye caught sight of his uniform. The man looked in his mid-twenties and wore a midnight blue suit with a white stripe down the sleeve. The black shirt he wore underneath his blazer meant he was undoubtedly a Sponsor. A wave of terror ran through Faye's body and her shoulders went stiff.

Turning back to her brother, she spoke in a hushed voice. "He's a Sponsor, we need to move now."

Dax ground his teeth together and hissed, "I know that Einstein, I was trying to tell you!"

Dax had barely finished his sentence when footsteps began to echo from down the street. At first they seemed slow, but gradually they gained pace growing nearer and nearer.

They stood up and moved away from the steps. As Faye began to turn toward the now running man, Dax grabbed her arm and pulled her away. His grip left marks on her skin and Faye noticed the wave of fear that passed over his face just before he tried to regain composure.

"Right, I'm going to run the opposite direction to you," Dax said, panic rising in his voice. "Meet me down the alley where I met you last Christmas." Dax started to turn, half sprinting away from Faye and shouted back, "If I don't turn up, grab a drink where the flag flies. Trust me."

His words reverberated round the empty space, and Faye turned in time to see Dax racing toward the advancing Sponsor. Knowing that if she waited any longer she would be removed for sure, Faye dashed toward the shadows and slipped down a blackened alleyway. Taking the steps at the end two at a time, she sprinted straight across the next road and jumped the fence into someone's garden. Landing with a thud on something cold and made of metal, she looked down to see she was lying on a patio table. The grooves pressed into her palms and she moved to fix the pain in her shoulder. Obviously her landing hadn't had the same grace as a gymnast's. She straightened up and took a moment to gather where she was.

You could hardly call it a garden because there wasn't one flower in sight. But then again, by those standards Covent Garden wasn't either. Most of the space was taken up by suburban looking furniture that sat upon varnished wooden decking. The house looked quite modern, but the lace curtains gave it away. It had obviously been bought as a gift for an older couple who didn't care for modern living.

Taking another look around more carefully this time, Faye noticed the furniture was rusting. Part of the varnish was beginning to peel away, exposing the woodwork underneath, and the fence panels were rotting. Funny how first appearances can often be misleading.

Faye walked over to the fence she had just jumped and some of the wood came away in her hand. Using her nails, she made a hole just big enough to see through in one panel. Faye cautiously surveyed her surroundings. She knew this area well and immediately settled on which connecting streets she could use to escape. But I shouldn't have to think of ways to escape! Faye thought to herself. I'm seventeen. I like reading, I like music, I'm normal. I shouldn't be running from people at one in the morning!

Deciding it was safe enough to retreat from the metal garden, Faye slowly hoisted herself over the fence and dropped to the pavement, landing badly on her ankle. Keeping low to the ground in case there were other Sponsors patrolling the streets, she began to head for their alley. It wasn't far from there and not particularly well lit; the perfect place for meeting in secret.

Last Christmas, she'd used the alley for very different reasons. Dax had asked to meet with her in private, so they'd found their alley after admiring the Covent Garden Christmas lights.

* * *

Last Christmas.

"Dax, why couldn't you just talk to me at home?" Faye asked, puzzled and slightly frustrated by her brother's secrecy.

"Close your eyes," Dax said, growing excitement in his voice. "Oh, and hold your hands out in front of you."

Scrunching her eyes as tight as they would close, she tentatively placed both hands in front of her. As Dax said, "No peeking," she felt something small drop into the palms of her hands. Feeling the object with her fingers, Faye caught one of them on a serrated edge. It seemed to be quite narrow at one end and wider at the other. A ring was attached to the wide end with a small indentation set into the object.

"Open your eyes," Dax said. "Merry Christmas and sorry I

missed your birthday ... and your results ... and pretty much everything else."

In Faye's hand was a key. But not just any key, a key to something she'd wanted for years.

"Dax, you got me a car?" Faye asked incredulously.

He looked at her cautiously, trying to test whether she was happy or not and replied, "Yes?"

"AHHH!" Faye screeched, throwing her arms around her now bewildered brother. "You got me a car! But it's sooo human, and you did it anyway, and ... and ..." It looked as if Faye was about to explode. "...cheers!"

Her excitement was momentarily interrupted when she looked sheepishly at her feet. "Oh, I kind of got you a ... magazine subscription," she admitted.

Dax looked at her for a moment, then began to laugh uncontrollably. He sat down against the brick wall, clutching his stomach and trying to fight back tears. Faye stopped, thought about how ridiculous she'd just sounded and couldn't help joining in.

For this one moment, Faye and Dax had been completely carefree. They'd felt so close, and for the first time in their lives, they'd considered themselves brother and sister. A rare occurrence indeed.

* * *

There were no lights now. Just the dark stretching out before her as she raced to find the hopeless brother she'd lost.

Watching for street names as she passed, Faye finally found the street she was looking for. Heather Gardens. At the end of this road was their alleyway.

Faye sped up as she neared the place where she hoped to find her brother waiting. Turning the corner, she stepped into the alley and found an empty space. He wasn't there.

Perhaps he got held up, Faye reasoned. After all, she'd had more time than him to reach it.

Glancing at her watch, she saw that it was half past one in the morning.

Faye walked over to the brick wall and sat down against it with her knees hugged close to her chest. The cold was biting now and she kind of wished she'd taken his gloves earlier. She'd wait for him.

Amy Durrant

She knew he'd come, Dax was made of strong stuff. Faye closed her eyes and waited for her brother to find her in the low light of their alley.

* * *

Faye could see daylight through the insides of her eyelids. It was morning and her brother would be in the alleyway asleep on her feet. She stretched out her shoulders and cracked the aches out of her back. Faye guessed that was to be expected having spent a night slumped against a wall in the freezing cold. She slowly opened her eyes and looked around. No-one. Dax wasn't there.

Fearing the worst, she tried to recall the second instruction he'd given her. Pausing for a moment to think, she remembered he'd said to go to the place where the flag flies. There must be hundreds of flags flying in London! Unfortunately, specifics had never really been Dax's strong point and as poignant as he'd thought his sentence had been, she had absolutely no idea how to get there.

Chapter 6
Clare Fynn

Clare gazed at the buildings that towered over her. They seemed to stretch on forever into the air with limitless height.

She didn't often visit this place and it frightened her to think about what went on behind the polished windows. It wasn't so much the people inside she was scared of, but the people they brought there.

The light reflected off her eyes, catching the quartz in her irises as she brushed her honey hair behind her ears. Clare, although she didn't like to admit it, was the daughter of notorious leader Torre Fynn and unlike her father, she was a hybrid. Thank God she wasn't like her father. If only he'd disappeared instead of her mother.

Her mother had been removed three years ago and not a day went by when Clare didn't think of her. She'd had the warmest smile; an odd match for Clare's cold hearted father.

Clare had no brothers or sisters and was constantly kept out of the public eye.

Her father had said, "It's nothing personal darling, you just might make me look bad, that's all."

She'd never got on with her father. He was one of those people that picked fights for the sake of it and won hands down. She didn't trust him either. Even when he'd placed her in the protection of two guards last summer, she knew it was to stop her from interfering in his election campaign.

Amy Durrant

* * *

Last Summer.

"Now Clare, I need you to behave yourself. I'm very close to winning this election and I'd like for you to be a part of it, but I can't trust you. You'll be safer in this locked prison cell anyway dear," Fynn grimaced. It might have passed for a smile, but the coldness is his eyes prevented it. "It's nothing personal darling, you just might make me look bad, that's all."

Clare stared on incredulously. "Well good luck winning an election without your manifesto document thing Torre ..." Clare teased her father and produced a leather bound book embroidered with silver thread.

Anger began to boil up from Fynn's toes and he lost all control as he leapt for the document, swiping Clare out of the way as he did so. Recovering his composure, Torre loomed over his daughter and barked at one of the guards to ready the cell. "You have just made a grave mistake, Clare," Torre growled, as he continued to advance toward the disinterested teenager. "You will regret challenging me, I can promise you that much. You will not see daylight for a very, very, long time."

One guard caught Clare loosely by the arm and her attempts at struggling were futile. "But daddy, I'll miss you," she added sarcastically, as she was led away. "Don't forget to come and visit!"

A big hunk of a man maneuvered Clare toward a black slate that moved aside to reveal its true form as a door. "Nice to meet you, I'm going to be your prison guard for the duration of your stay."

Clare glared at the man. "What, you can't afford to work out? You've got so much extra weight on your arms, look at that!"

The guard clearly didn't appreciate Clare's snideness and shoved her into the room, slamming the door firmly shut.

"You could at least give me a book to read!" Clare proposed. There were ten minutes worth of silence and pacing until a hatch opened above her and a square object fell from the ceiling onto the floor with a loud thud.

To satisfy her burning curiosity, Clare picked up what turned out to be a book with the title Torre Fynn: How to reach the top.

"Oh I get it, very funny. I'm sure I'd love to read a book written by my dad. Oh no wait, he didn't write any of it! He hired someone to do it for him."

The hatch opened again and the guard's face peered down at the girl who was twirling hair between her fingertips. "You're going to be in here a while kid. So shut up and make yourself comfy."

***

Grinding her teeth together, Clare began to walk toward the familiar main complex, a slight skip in her step. It was a large square tower, with one entrance and one exit. A stranger might've mistaken it for a prison; Clare had learnt this the hard way. Sponsors and guards patrolled the area every hour of the day and there was more than enough security. Not that the Lamplight particularly needed the security, it was practically an impenetrable fortress anyway.

Technically she knew she shouldn't be here, but she had ways of working round the guards. All she had to do was approach one of the Sponsors and they'd take care of the rest.

To the untrained eye, Clare could've looked like a hitchhiker, wearing striped pink and green knee high socks with a light brown dress. On her back was a fair sized rucksack and round her neck she wore a matching pink and green scarf.

Clare was sixteen years old, but nearing her seventeenth birthday. She'd never been spoilt and could completely take care of herself. Or at least, she liked to think she could.

Continuing to calmly walk toward the tower that loomed in front of her, she saw one of the guards raise some sort of alarm. The only entrance was barred as a shutter fell across it, and the man ahead began to sprint. What an awful lot of effort to go to for one little girl, she thought.

She grinned and stood with her arms outstretched by her sides. "Come and get me boys," Clare taunted. She closed her eyes and imagined the sunset to keep herself calm. It would hurt less if she didn't resist so much and she'd been through this process many times before.

She heard shouting around her and someone calling for back up. Do I really look that much of a threat? she thought.

Then abruptly, the shouting stopped and she felt a stinging sensation in her neck. The light began to fade and she felt several pairs of strong arms lifting her, carrying her closer to her father. Clare smiled again and let herself fall willingly into a deep sleep.

* * *

Lark blinked, and gradually began to open his eyes. He was in a different room. He was wearing new clothes.

Okay now that's weird, he thought to himself. I object to being unwillingly undressed, especially in ominous tower blocks.

Starting to sit up, Lark cracked his knuckles and looked around. He was on a four poster bed surrounded by numerous chairs and benches, all draped with velvet looking material. The colors were still very neutral but the room was much more lavish than the one he'd been placed in earlier. In one of the corners, a man sat bolt upright watching him.

"Oh," Lark said hesitantly. His voice sounded harsher and deeper than he'd intended it to, with an adult ring to it. "Hi. Could you tell me where I am or something?"

The man he addressed cocked his head slightly, then stood up and walked out of the room. There was being rude and being bang out of order, and Lark thought this man was definitely the latter.

On the wall opposite him, Lark saw a full length mirror with a dressing table to the side of it. Lowering his legs over the edge of the bed, Lark began to stand but lost balance as he tried to grip one of the four posters. When he did, the wood nearly cracked with the force of his grip.

"What the ...?" he whispered to himself. Trying again, this time Lark successfully stood and found motion in his legs that carried him to the mirror. It felt like he'd been smashed over the head with some kind of bat repeatedly and his neck itched like crazy. Placing both hands on the wall either side of the mirror, Lark raised his head and stared at his reflection.

A pair of bright opal eyes set deep into their sockets glared back at him. The man had a short mop of pure white hair that spiked off in different directions. He had a square pronounced jaw line and wore some kind of uniform.

Trying to piece together how it had happened, Lark realized the reflection was definitely him. It moved the same way he did and reacted in the same way, but Lark looked so much, older.

Prisms

Looking down at his body, Lark saw a white open necked T-shirt with a black stripe down both of the short sleeves. He was also dressed in a pair of tight black jeans and black trainers.

This can't be me, I look too grown up. Lark thought. There were new muscles across his chest and stubble sat on his chin. Turning again to the mirror, Lark ran one of his hands through his new mop of hair and sank to a crouch in disbelief. He dropped his head into his hands just as the door began to open.

"Lark," Fynn remarked, "great to see you up and about." There was something ever so conceited about his voice and he walked further into the room, flanked by two guards and sat down in one of the velvet chairs. Straightening out of his crouch, Lark moved toward the leader and pulled a chair opposite him.

Fynn smiled lightly and said, "Our world is changing. Our people seem to grow restless when the conference intervenes and we need to fix that."

Lark sat in complete silence, watching the man with wary eyes. A hatch opened above him but he didn't dare take his eyes off Fynn. The man had less charm than a rattlesnake and all the warmth of crocodile.

"Our Sponsorship program is no longer adequate, and—" He was cut short as another guard entered the room and bowed before him.

"Sir my apologies for the interruption, but I regret to inform you we have your daughter being held in one of the cells."

It was hard to miss the annoyance in Fynn's face. "Why is Clare being held in a cell? Is she in any trouble?" It was more like a statement than a question, as Fynn knew all too well the types of stunts his daughter liked to pull.

Lark's interest perked. He'd never seen Torre's daughter but if she was anything like her father, he didn't think he'd never want to meet her.

The guard shifted nervously on the spot and replied, "We found her on the grounds, and ..." he paused briefly. "...she hasn't woken up yet."

Fynn looked at Lark for a moment as he considered his options, then barked, "Bring her here. Perhaps she'd like to meet the future face of the conference."

Amy Durrant

* * *

Make a mental note to try and not to do that so often, Clare reminded herself. She knew that if she wanted something she'd find a way of getting it, but for the love of Mara did it hurt! Clare twisted her neck round, trying to shake off the after-burn from the clipper.

After blacking out she'd ended up in one of the holding cells. It looked like a bleak waiting room and usually she was in the transition suite. It was obviously already occupied by someone else this time.

Clare stood up and continued to rub the side of her neck. She'd forgotten how much it stung to have your birth mark clipped. They might as well taser you, that was practically what it was anyway.

Searching the room, she found what she was looking for. Dragging the chair to the centre of the room, she stood on it and shouted "Hey, I'm Clare Fynn and I'll be your prisoner for the duration of my stay. Nice to meet you!" There was no response, so she continued, "At least last time I got a book to read, you cutting back on your spending?"

She waited for a moment then a door opened above her.

A man glared down at her. "Charming as ever Clare. I'm surprised you haven't been thrown in here sooner. I remember your antics from last time."

She twisted a lock of hair round her finger and replied, "Well, you know what they say, elephants never forget."

The door slammed shut and another opened in the side of the wall. A guard stepped into the room. He was very bulky, the type who could probably withstand being dropped from the top of a very large tower. Clare had contemplated testing this before.

The guard's eyes were burning. "Mr. Fynn requests you see him immediately," he ordered.

Clare looked up into her thinking space, jumped off the chair and joked, "Actually, I quite like this room. I think I'll stay here." She sat down on the chair in the middle of the room and smiled sweetly at the guard as she crossed her arms and legs. He couldn't touch her. She could keep this up all day and she'd still be in control.

The man lumbered forward and took Clare roughly by the top of her shoulder. He pulled her to the door. "I have no objection to dragging you there and I'm sure Mr. Fynn won't notice if you turn up a little bruised," he threatened.

Clare looked at him in disgust and tried to shake free his arm. Eventually he let go, and motioned for her to walk in front of him. In an act of spite, she stuck her tongue out at her favorite guard and marched forwards.

* * *

Lark rubbed his jaw and trailed both hands down the arms of the chair.

On learning of his daughter's arrival, Fynn had decided to postpone their conversation until she was in the same room.

The guards shifted nervously at the walls and kept their gaze at their feet.

What was it with people in this place? thought Lark. Can't they even bring themselves to look Fynn in the eye? To be honest, though, he was incredibly intimidating and highly unstable, so that probably had something to do with it.

Lark's thoughts were interrupted when a girl stormed into the room and threw the door open.

"Darling!" Fynn greeted. "Nice of you to drop in on us, take a seat over there next to Lark." He went to hug the girl but she ducked under one of his arms.

"Lark, this is my delightful daughter, Clare." There was no sincerity in his voice, just formality; like he was obliged to say it to keep up appearances. She was nothing like Lark had imagined. Lark looked at her trying to guess her age and thought she might've been a year older than him. Studying her rose tinted eyes, Lark looked down at the ground, embarrassed by the way she'd stared back. Then he saw her glance in horror at his neck. Reaching for the place her eyes were fixated on, Lark only felt the newly formed pattern. Damn, he thought, I forgot to check that earlier.

Fynn relaxed back in his chair again and restarted their previous conversation. "What I'm about to say relates directly to you Lark, but the consequences will affect you." He gestured toward Clare. "And a small, insignificant percentage of the population.

"The Sponsors control the majority of movement through the Lamplight but groups like your resistance have made it impossible for them to maintain control." Fynn's eyes grew dark and Clare saw danger in his face. Lark shifted nervously in his chair but tried not to let his unease show.

"We are replacing them with Runners. You, Lark, are the first of this kind," Fynn continued.

Lark looked confused, and turned to see if Clare shared the same facial expression as he did. Instead, her eyes were cold, as if she was accusing him of committing some terrible crime.

"We think we have found the cause of this problem," Fynn said. His voice was deadly serious and his face grave. "Since experiments are causing the problem, we have a solution. A water-tight solution."

Lark stared at the leader dumbfounded, and asked in horror, "By experiments, you mean half Marans half Humans, am I correct?" Clare looked at her father with glazed eyes. Lark wanted desperately to comfort the girl but turned back to Fynn, awaiting his response.

"Yes, I do." Clare's face dropped and she leapt from the chair, dashing for the door. Fynn nodded once and the guard caught her in a tight vice, refusing to let her go. She tried to break free but had to stop fighting against the guard's iron grip, knowing it was pointless to even try to escape.

Fynn stared straight at Lark and carried on with the conversation as if Clare's outburst hadn't happened. "The Runners will become a new race of people. They will be strong, powerful, agile and virtually invincible. The conference will issue a law next week prohibiting people from traveling through the Lamplight and it will be the Runner's job to ensure this is enforced.

"The marking on your neck Lark, will enable you to access this complex as and when you need to. As experiments are the only people who can easily pass through the Lamplight, you must remove anyone who tries." Fynn placed a great deal of emphasis on the word 'anyone' and Lark saw Clare's jaw drop in horror. For once in his life, Lark was absolutely speechless.

"No travel from Earth to Mara unless I approve it, no second chances for those who disobey. You will replace the Sponsors and order WILL be restored to the streets of both worlds."

Clare's legs buckled underneath her, and she looked to the guard for support. He held her like a rag doll and picked her limp body up so she was again standing on her feet.

"How will I have the power to ... remove people?" Lark hated to say it out loud, and despised the idea of him being involved in something so cruel and heartless.

Fynn stood up and motioned to one of the guards. After whispering something in his ear, the guard left briefly and returned with something which he placed into Fynn's hands.

Fynn then walked toward Lark and gave him a metal rod. On one end there was a small prism, and on the other was a wrist strap so the user could attach it to their arm.

"This," Fynn said pointing to the rod, "is an eraser." He circled Lark once then returned to sitting in his chair. "If you catch a hybrid attempting to travel between two worlds, you apply this to the mark on their neck and a flash of light is all it will take for you to remove someone without even pulling a trigger.

"Guns are outdated and we've found the erasers to be much more ... effective."

Clare struggled against the arms of her captor and screamed. "You monster! You're dirt, you're nothing!" Then she spat on the ground by her father.

He looked at her in contempt and demanded, "Take Clare to a comfortable cell. Make sure she has a good view, I expect she'll be spending some time there." The guard complied and half dragged, half carried her away while she screamed, "I hate you! I have no father, you're dead to me!"

Lark stared after her in disbelief then looked back at Fynn. His eyes were like glass and not one flicker of emotion could be seen on his face.

"I'm glad you understand," he addressed Lark. "I'm sure you realize the importance of your role and the part you have to play in the weeks to come."

Lark bit down on his tongue to stop himself from screaming at the collected leader. This man was dangerous, but worse still, he had the resources to support him. Lark knew he had no choice but to comply and while he wasn't afraid of death, he didn't want to die today. He could at least help that girl first. "Thank you. If that's all, I'd like you to show me out," Lark said through gritted teeth.

Fynn nodded. "Of course. But, before you go, I'd like you to help me with something." Lark didn't respond, so he continued. "A member of the conference, Mr. Link, disappeared about one week ago. Now, a Sponsor of ours recently apprehended his son Dax but due to unfortunate circumstances we lost him."

Something in Lark's eyes registered when Fynn said the name Dax, but he couldn't place where he knew it from.

"Link has a daughter called Anna; she also goes by the name Faye. We know that currently she's somewhere in London and it is our number one priority we find her before someone else does. It shouldn't be too hard as we are monitoring the Lamplight and will be informed if she passes between worlds. We believe she has something very valuable in her possession that could compromise the entire operation." Fynn's eyes grew dark and he leant ever so slightly forward in his chair. The sudden movement took Lark by surprise and he flinched. A thin smile spread across the leader's face. It was clear he enjoyed inciting fear.

Lark nodded and replied, "Of course. I'll try my best to bring her in."

Fynn looked troubled. "She can't be brought here, not yet. What you need to do is befriend her, gain her trust, do whatever it takes. When she believes you are still a member of the resistance, you must bring her to me unharmed. Throughout this task, it is vital that Faye does not know you are a Runner."

Lark stood up and half bowed to Fynn like he'd seen other guards doing. "I won't fail you," he said. His face tried to look sure, but his wavering voice gave him away.

Lark turned and began to walk toward the door. As he did this, Fynn shouted, "Oh, and Lark?" Lark stopped, waiting to hear what Fynn had to say.

"If you do fail, it won't just be your position you lose."

Chapter 7
Trix of the Trade

Kash had only ever been lost once in her life. When she was seven, her parents had taken her and Lark to Centar as a treat. She'd scored ten out of ten on a spelling test, and they couldn't just leave Lark at home, so they'd brought him along with them.

It had been mid cold season and the air was turning crisp from the mild heat of the season high. The sun was beginning to pass behind the shaded clouds and one after another, the streets lamps began to flicker into life.

Her mother's hand was smooth and a perfect fit for Kash's own miniature palm. She'd promised she wouldn't let go and Kash felt safe in the embrace of her mother. She could feel the warmth from her skin, as her body temperature failed to change quick enough.

People rushed past in dark suits, as coats wearing shiny buttons and thousands of trousers moving at many hundreds of mile an hour. To Kash, this was grown up world. She didn't really belong there; she was so tiny in comparison.

Her father grinned, swung Lark round into a big hug and said, "Who wants some hot chocolate?" This was a real treat. Chocolate was imported from Earth and the artificial stuff tasted horrible and grainy. Real chocolate was priceless and Kash loved nothing better than drinking a cup of it as big as her head.

Kash's adult memory had forgotten exactly what happened next, but she remembered sitting on a step in the middle of a busy street. She remembered tears rolling down her cheeks and falling to the ground in little droplets. She felt so lonely and lost. Why has mother left me? she'd thought.

But mother had been away from home before and Kash had created something that took the place in her heart when she left. Ever since she'd created it, Kash had carried it with her everywhere.

Reaching a small hand into one of her pockets, seven year old Kash fumbled with something and pulled out a tiny white paper bird. Cradling it in her hands, she pinched it beneath the fragile wings and moved her arm, as if the bird was swooping and soaring on the wind.

The little bird didn't feel lonely. It was happy because it was free to fly where it wanted and could meet with lots of other little birds. So while Kash was truly alone for the first time, she was content where she was.

Kash didn't remember much after that. She vaguely recalled some sort of reuniting with her parents, but couldn't describe it in much detail. Unfortunately, her memories seemed to grow cloudier the older she got.

Dax being lost wasn't quite the same, but Kash wished she could curl into a ball and find another paper bird to ease her misery. It was never that easy though, was it?

It had taken her barely two minutes to reach Centar from Hem and the rail had been surprisingly empty. Not one shady looking man in a trench coat in sight. Now she was here, truth be told Kash didn't really know where to start looking.

The shops were almost closing and the people began to disperse, so she knew she had to think quickly. Okay, she addressed her mind, where is the one place I know Dax visited regularly? Trying to gather any clues that would lead her to a friend of Dax, Kash only remembered him ever talking about one shop. The same shop where they'd first met.

Knowing the exact route to take, she set off at a lightning pace. Now she was the grown up racing along in her childhood world. Trying to solve Dax's mysterious disappearance reminded Kash of an old Earthly puzzle. It was as if Dax was at the centre of a Rubik's Cube. The small squares were the people Dax knew, the bright colors matching their hair and eyes. They could be moved in an infinite number of ways, but to get to Dax, Kash would have to find a way of rearranging the colors until she found a match.

She smiled to herself as this analogy lingered in her mind and abruptly stopped in front of an aging shop. A vivid blue chair sat outside, and the woodwork round the windows was weathered where it had been beaten and roughed by the wind. The place where she'd first met Dax.

The shop had been running for over seventy years. In Maran terms, that was practically forever. Kash ascended the worn steps and went to push the door, just as she noticed the closed sign. A light was doused inside and she could see the silhouette of a hunched figure on the back wall.

"Hello!" Kash shouted, banging on the door and peering through the circular pane. "Hello, Mr. Simms! I really need to talk to you!"

Kash heard movement inside and a voice called back. "I know, I know, you're different and if you don't buy what you came for your world will end etcetera. Now, if you don't mind, I've had a busy day so I'm going to bed."

Kash hit the door in frustration. "Please, I just need a minute." She was starting to sound desperate and tears formed in the corners of her eyes. "My fiancé, I've got to find him, he's gone and ... and ..." Kash was now half crying on the steps of the shop. "...and I think I've lost Dax." She knew how much of a sorry sight she must look.

There was no reply from behind the other side of the door, so Kash turned and sunk to the step, tears matting in the fringe of her hair. As she considered going home, there was movement inside the shop.

The door behind her creaked open and an old voice asked, "Did you say, Dax?"

Kash looked up in disbelief and stood to face the old man. He himself looked about eighty years old and thin wispy hair sat upon his balding head. His eyes were crinkled and wise, and his cheeks wrinkled from the many years of smiling to customers. Now his face was curious but also troubled as he gazed at the girl.

"Thank you!" Kash wailed, and flung her arms around the old man. Unsure of what to do next, the man stood there taken aback by this sudden act of thanks. Kash dried her eyes with the back of her hand and released the shop keeper. "Sorry," she apologized, aware she had just thrown herself on an elderly member of the population.

"That's Okay, it happens all the time." The man smiled in reassurance and Kash felt slightly less like she'd just assaulted him. "I think you'd best come inside," he suggested.

Kash stepped through the door and stared in amazement at the half lit shop of 'Simms and Sons'. It was like a treasure trove of odd objects, a traditional curio shop. There were contraptions from beyond her wildest dreams and objects she presumed must've come from Earth.

Old shelves lined with dusty books, an antique English telephone sat on the desk with a large bell alarm clock next to it. Picture frames housing oddly dressed men and women from places like France and England cluttered one table and another was full of tiny jars that contained what Kash thought were sweets. All the items looked typically human, old and absolutely original.

She walked over to one cabinet and reached to open it, when the man said, "Whatever it is you want to know, I probably know it." The man reached for an old wooden pipe with beautiful patterns carved into it and began puffing away. The blue smoke quickly filled the small shop and collected in rings around the dim halos of recently lit candlelight. "I am Riley Simms, owner and proprietor of this little shop. I have been for nearly fifty years now and my head is a bank of memories dating back to times when you weren't even born."

Turning her attention away from the cabinet, she looked at him in wonder, wanting to hear one of his tales but reminding herself of the real reason she was there.

"Mr. Simms, I ..." Kash began to ask when the man interjected.

"Please call me Riley, Mr. Simms was my father."

Kash smiled politely and corrected herself. "Riley. I haven't seen Dax in a while and can't seem to find him. I thought perhaps you might've seen him?"

Riley thought about this for a second, then spoke in a quiet voice. "You mean Link, yes?"

Kash shook her head fervently and waited.

"You don't want to go asking something like that to any old people now, love. You don't know what secrets they may be hiding, or who they might be."

Kash looked at him slightly embarrassed and he continued. "There have been rumors, stories, about people disappearing, all because they were in the wrong place at the wrong time or talked to the wrong people. If you go around asking people outright questions like that, don't be surprised if you go disappearing too."

It was more like a friendly warning than a threat, but Kash's eyes still widened with fear.

"You're okay with me love," Riley grinned. "It's just some others might not be as plain and honest as myself."

Kash nodded and relaxed a little. After all, she didn't have much to worry about talking to an eighty year old man who could barely walk. She straightened herself and asked again, "So, have you seen him then?"

Riley hobbled to the cash desk and sat down in an antique leather chair. The arms were worn and the color fading, turning darker green, but Kash guessed that must be why it was called antique. "I haven't seen that much of our Dax lately. He came in about four days ago to have a chat; wanted to know if any weird customers with a funny looking scar on their neck had come into the shop."

Kash's face fell as she began to think she'd hit a dead end already. Her emerald eyes looked to the floor and she heaved a sigh of disappointment. "Did he say where he was going next?" Kash asked regardless.

The old man thought about her question for some time, or perhaps he'd just not heard her properly and then said, "Actually, he did mention some place he was going. Visiting someone ... now who was it?"

Kash fell impatient. She quite clearly didn't know the answer. Dax had taken off very suddenly in the night without even so much as a goodbye. She was going to kill him when she found him.

"Oh, that's right!" Kash's eyes flicked to the man in anticipation. "He was visiting his sister, oh what's her name. Faye? Frieda? Freddie?"

The name didn't register with Kash so she asked, "Does Dax have two sisters then? I know he has one sister called Anna."

Riley stared at her for a moment and chuckled. "You really don't know that much about his family now do you. Anna is her first name, but she never uses it, hates it you see. I'm pretty sure she goes by Faye now I come to think of it."

"Brilliant," Kash said. "Thanks for all your help." As she turned to walk out, she remembered. "Oh, where could I find Faye?"

Riley looked unsure whether she was being serious or not.

"Well if she's not here, she's in London of course!"

Kash looked at him with cold eyes. "But I can't travel through the Lamplight, how am I going to get to her?!"

The man closed his eyelids and lay back in the chair, resting his head against one of the many bookshelves. "I can't help you there love," the man apologized. "But however you get there, do it quickly. I would if them rumors are true."

Kash tilted her head, trying to recall if he'd actually told her the rumors. "What rumors?"

Riley opened his eyes again. "If what's been said on the wire is correct, the Lamplight will close in one week. Would've thought a bright young spark like you would already have heard that?"

Kash still didn't understand. She shook her head and asked, "What does that mean for me exactly?"

Riley sat upright. "You don't reach this girl in a week? Lights out."

Chapter 8
Faces of Fury

Everyone knew how the system worked. Once on the Sponsors' radar, you were unlikely to drop off it. Faye wasn't stupid enough to go home. If they'd thought Dax had been involved in illegal activities, her house would've been turned over by now. She just hoped her mother had been treated well and that the Sponsors had decided not to involve her. Faye thought it unlikely.

It was a struggle for her to even pin point what she'd done wrong. No resistance had recruited her and she'd remained neutral ever since the worldly leaders had come to power. Not one of her school teachers could've said a bad word against her and she'd treated the Lamplight with nothing but respect.

Although now, she was starting to question if she'd played a part in it all along. Father was missing, so was Dax and she couldn't even contact her mother. But, maybe she was just being over paranoid. An undeniable family trait that she couldn't possibly have hoped to escape. How much trouble could she really be in though, just for staying out a bit past bed time? The conference had much bigger issues to deal with and she was convinced she wasn't one of them.

Since waking in the alleyway, Faye had walked around the streets for a while and ended up down a small road with a pub on the end. The only people who went to pubs now were students, or members of the conference with a death wish.

Faye's wrist clock told her it was midday, but it felt much later and the sun had made way for thick banks of grey cloud that rolled over London.

There was no particular reason to head back through the Lamplight, so Faye thought it was best if she remained in London for Dax to find her. She wasn't exactly sure how he'd do that, but her tenacious brother always seemed to find a way. The clouds rumbled and threatened to throw it down. Faye brushed the hair from her face and quickened her walking pace before she got caught in the storm.

Sponsors very rarely patrolled the quiet streets during the day. It was at night, when the rebels came out, that they switched from the busy crowds to the suburban cul-de-sacs.

With this in mind, Faye hurried toward the pub at the end of the road. It was charmingly called "The Barrel and Barman" and looked perhaps a century old. No one lingered outside making small talk, and there were no tables or chairs to tempt them to either. Faye pushed the old door and it creaked open slowly, protesting against its hinges.

Inside, twenty or so faces peered at Faye with cautious eyes. Many were human, although there were about two hybrids sat among them, equally as suspicious as the others. All twenty appeared to be students and sat in silence drinking beer from a pint glass. They were all male and while that didn't frighten Faye, what did was the way they stared at her with murderous eyes.

Faye kept her own crimson eyes down and shuffled toward the bar. She had little change in her pocket and searched to find enough to order a drink.

The bartender, a man in his late thirties with a bald head and gruff voice asked, "What do you want?"

Faye sat at the bar, focusing on the beer mat in front of her and said, "Nothing."

Sniggers could be heard around her and the barman slammed a fist down where her eyes were fixed. "If you're not going to order anything, you can leave."

Faye glanced up for the first time and virtually whispered, "I've not got any money on me." It felt to her as if she was a mouse playing steel drums on the teeth of a lion. But to be honest, Faye didn't care. She didn't care if he threw her out and she didn't particularly care if the students leapt up and attacked her. Well, maybe she cared a little about being attacked. Her mind was too troubled to worry about anything other than how her world could be shattering so quickly.

The fist in front of her relaxed a little and Faye looked up to see pity in the man's face. This was the face of a father, not a thug. Obviously he'd decided she wasn't much of a threat. He leant forward and placed a pint of water in front of her. Faye couldn't understand what the man was trying to achieve. Was he mocking her? As she stared at the ice cold water, condensation forming in tiny droplets on the outside of the glass, she realized she was parched.

She fixed her eye on another point on the bar to take her mind off the thirst, and the stocky bartender announced, "Just drink it."

Faye wasn't entirely sure if he was serious. A virtual lie detector, she scanned his face and decided he was being honest. Clasping her hands around the cool surface of the glass she said, "Thanks."

The water looked so refreshing, so she lifted it to her dry lips. It soothed her throat, like water quenching a flaming fire. There was some muttering around her and the students began to slowly engage in conversation with one another.

Faye relaxed somewhat and turned on her stool to face the television that was quietly playing away in the corner.

It was hard to hear it, so deciding it was probably safe to ask, she turned to the barman and said, "Umm, could you turn up that TV please? It looks like the news is on." The bartender grunted and reached for the remote. As he turned up the volume, the hum of the students' conversations seemed to also grow louder.

On the TV, a smart looking news reporter said, "Good afternoon, I'm Sash Evans with the latest story. The conference broadcast their latest development this afternoon in the fight to tackle illegal transport through the Lamplight. We received this broadcast only minutes ago from Torre Fynn at the complex."

Faye strained against the noise to hear the reporter. Forgetting her surroundings, she shouted, "Will you just shut up a sec!"

If there had been any doubt whether the students wanted to attack Faye before, there was none left now. Faye glared at the TV screen, visibly annoyed but attempting to become as invisible as possible. She could feel pairs of eyes boring into her but at that moment, all her attention was focused on the box in the corner.

Torre Fynn came onto the screen, sat in a lavish office behind a polished wooden desk. His hands were clasped in front of him and he addressed the camera.

"Citizens of Earth and Mara. When I was elected to worldly leader, I made you promises that I swore I would keep. One of these was a promise to maintain order in our streets and I have failed you. But now, I have the opportunity to rectify the situation. As of one week today, I will be removing the Sponsorship program."

There was a brief silence in the pub, then all the students stood, cheering and shouting at the top of their lungs, "Death to the Sponsors!" The whole pub was alive and everyone in it temporarily united. Faye kept her eyes fixed on the screen, straining to hear the speech. The barman turned the volume up further and the now standing students turned to watch the rest of the broadcast, jubilation and triumph in their faces.

"In place of this, I will be introducing a more effective and efficient solution." The faces of the pub turned grave and slowly the students began to sit again. There was no shouting now.

"There will be a new breed of security. A new race of elite enforcers. They are called, the Runners." A deathly silence descended across the pub. Not one smile among them, not one face pleased.

"It became apparent to me a few months ago that there was much illegal activity connected to the Lamplight and much resistance to the law. There will be no room for negotiation. To break the law, is to defy the system. By breaking our law put in place to protect society, you will be declaring yourself a terrorist of the state. The law to be imposed in one week's time, will restrict all movement between worlds through the lamplight.

"Mara and Earth will be connected through the conference alone. Any persons who violate this law shall be removed without trial. I must, however, remind you that this is the worst case scenario. This law should hopefully only apply to a handful of the population and I would like to remind you it is for your own protection. Any unauthorized travel shall be seen as an act of terrorism. I thank you for your cooperation in our time of change and wish every citizen a long and happy future on their world."

No one spoke. The students stared on past the TV in disbelief and Faye felt she'd lost the ability to speak. Her family would be torn apart.

As this information began to register among the students, their silence turned to anger. They began to pick up glasses and hurl them at the television. They cursed and shouted in rage about the new law, and talked of revolution and murder. There was passion in their eyes, but it was dangerous. It was the passion of criminals and not of revolutionaries.

Faye ducked to avoid a flying glass that narrowly missed her head and instead shattered the mirror behind the bar. Shards flew off in every direction and showered the pub with tiny pieces of its own reflection.

The barman grabbed Faye by the arm and dragged her up the pub stairs. She was too shocked to react or resist, so didn't even question the man's actions. Anywhere but here was by far the safer option.

He looked at her seriously. "Stay in this bedroom for now. This lot are going mental and I don't want a kid down there."

Faye stood in shock on the landing. It was as if everything was a blur and she didn't know whether to shout or cry.

"Do you understand?" The barman stared at Faye and then virtually carried her into one of the upstairs rooms. "I'm going to lock the door," he shouted over the students' racket. "I will unlock it when they've calmed down, but I'm doing this for your own safety. If you leave this room, you will be taking your life into your own hands."

The barman hurried out and Faye heard the click of the lock as it slid firmly into place. Shouts and hollers could be heard from downstairs and the sound of sirens getting closer in the distance. She lay back on the bed and closed her eyes, waiting for the apocalypse to begin.

Chapter 9
Never Trust a Lyre

Torre Fynn was a murderer. At least, that was what Clare had decided. He was brutal and heartless and spineless, sending others off to carry out his dirty work. And what about that man Lark? How old was he? Dragged into this violent new regime and now he was the shiny head of Torre's spear. A tool, or weapon, to be used as and when by the conference.

"I will escape, you know!" Clare shouted, hoping that at least one of the guards had heard her. "Shame this door's loose ..." There was still no response. She was running out of convincing things to shout at the guards.

Clare paced round the door less room and kicked one of the walls. Her brain reminded her it would be pretty difficult escaping when there wasn't even a window that opened.

Argh! she thought. I hate the Lamplight! The room was black and white. No colors in between, no room for imagination. She was even wearing the same clothes as earlier because she refused to change into the depressing uniform she'd been given. There was one large-ish bed, one chair, one desk and one mirror in the room. In another part there was a screened off bathroom.

Clare was literally a prisoner of her father's complex. He couldn't just keep her here like this; it was against her human rights! But Clare knew what he'd say. "Darling, I just don't want you to get into trouble, that's all." Sitting in a big chair, looking all smug and powerful.

And where was Jonathon Caine? Torre had probably persuaded

him to take as little responsibility as possible. The entire major decision making was left to Mr. Fynn, the more suitable leader. He was very good at manipulating people like that.

Clare didn't have a clue what was going on in the outside world. She'd wanted to see her father to complain about the Sponsors. Now, she was trapped in a cell with an even bigger complaint. If the Runners truly were immortal, then all hybrids didn't stand a chance. Including her, she reminded herself.

It was so boring sitting in a room doing nothing, but sitting there made her think about her mother and if she'd ever been in the same position.

Fynn had removed her mother following an outrageous scandal. Her mother had been the leader of the largest resistance group on the planet when Fynn had been elected. The two greatest enemies married to each other, living under the same roof. Fynn had said it had been "bad for publicity." That was his only reasoning for removing her mother.

Clare loved her a thousand times more than she did her father and although she hadn't told anyone, she upheld all the ideals of the resistance. She was her mother's girl and that was what made Fynn so angry. Every time he looked at Clare, he saw the person who'd betrayed him. He didn't have time for a "pathetic low-life intent on ruining him." That was the kind of talk reserved for strictly behind closed doors, out of the public eye.

Focusing back to the situation at hand, Clare decided that her best plan of action was to find a gap where the door should be. Then when she left the Lamplight, although she wasn't sure how to now her prism had been confiscated, she would join any resistance left standing and give them all the Intel necessary to take down her father.

There were so many places where the door could've been! She ran her hands over the bleached walls for at least one hour before she gave up. It was like searching for a rock in a rock pool. Clare walked to the black bed and lay back, closing her eyes. When she drifted to sleep, her dreams were disturbed with flashes of gunfire and screaming. It woke her abruptly and she didn't dare try to sleep again. Instead, she gazed out at the polished towers.

The annoying thing about the Lamplight was that there was no weather or seasons. No sun or moon, or changing time of day. Essentially, everything remained the same; frozen in a flawed pocket of reality. Clare twisted a lock of hair round her finger and sighed.

The wrist clock she wore told her it was now Tuesday. Six days left before the Runners came. Then, quite unexpectedly, a door opened in front of her. She hadn't even prized it open, it simply slid to one side offering itself up as a way out.

A man strode through a gap in the opposite wall in an open necked shirt, trousers and shoes all colored black. It was a sharp contrast to his pure white hair. He hurried inside and shut the door behind him. The lines where it had been, disappeared and once again it was a blank wall.

"What did you do that for?" she hollered at him. "How am I going to get out now you've lost the door?!"

Lark sauntered over and sat on the end of the bed. "Planning a daring escape are we?" he smirked.

"Don't test me," Clare threatened. "I know self defense."

Lark held his hands up. "Wow. Self defense on a guy who's invincible. You'll get sooo far," he joked.

Clare made a noise of disgust. "If you've come here to mock, then just leave. I expect pretty boy has lots of things to do now. Besides, I don't keep company with idiots," she announced proudly. She crossed her arms and looked away.

Lark nodded. "Aww, as much as that hurts me, it's probably true. But I'm the idiot with the key."

Clare looked up at him confused, unsure if he wanted to help or taunt her. She decided it was probably a mixture of the two.

"Go on," Clare said, sitting up and pretending to look only marginally interested. "I suppose I can spare some time to listen to you."

Lark grinned and continued. "Okay. What I'm about to do is probably illegal, but I want to help."

Wow, this guy was even more of an idiot than Clare had first presumed. She laughed and began to pace, circling Lark and then sitting calmly on the edge of the bed. "You. Want to help me?"

Clearly her confidence unnerved and fascinated Lark at the same time, because he leant casually back against a wall. "Well, I'm invincible. I may as well help if I can't be killed. All that talk by your dad about 'It won't just be your position you lose' is just a load of tough talk. I'm stronger than him."

Prisms

Clare didn't think arrogance suited this guy, but today he seemed to be wearing it like a jacket. "Okay, do what," she snapped. Clare looked at her nails and began to examine them as if bored.

Noticing this, Lark asked, "Well, if you don't want me to rescue you, I'll leave then." He got up and began to walk back toward the blank wall.

"Wait!" Clare shouted. He stopped mid step and turned round. "Firstly, does it look like I need rescuing?" Lark contemplated this but before he could answer, Clare said, "No, I don't. That was a rhetorical question."

A smirk spread across Lark's face. Look at him, looking all smug and stupid, Clare thought. "And secondly, assuming you could rescue me," she mimicked Lark's voice, "why would you do that?"

Realizing he'd caught her attention, Lark smiled. "Because apart from you being utterly charming and very pretty ..." Clare snorted as he said this, glaring at him with a face that said, 'I'm totally unimpressed'. Lark continued regardless, "I don't think it's fair you're kept locked up here and I thought in return, you could help me."

Clare didn't understand. "What could I possibly help you with? After all you're 'invincible'," she said, mimicking his voice.

"I want some help finding Faye and despite your attempts to hide it, I know about you wanting to join the resistance." Lark knew he was reeling Clare in.

"How did you ...?"

"...Know?" Lark interrupted. "You're darling father told me. You know, he's not as unobservant as you think. It seems you're very streetwise and know a thing or two about the resistance on Earth. I want you to come with me to track down Faye."

Clare considered this. "How do I know I can trust you?"

Lark smirked again and began tracing his hand along the edge of the bed. "You don't."

Clare stared at him in dismay, trying to work out why she should go with the newly turned Runner. "Forgive me for saying so, but I don't really care about finding this girl and you're probably a maniac! Why on Mara would I come with you?"

Lark stood up and stretched out one hand to Clare. "Because I can offer you protection from the Runners and get your stuff back. Oh and," he added, mimicking her voice, "I'm the idiot with the key."

Chapter 10
The Price Faye Pays

Faye felt restless. It had taken the bartender the remainder of the day to bring his pub to order again. It was 2.00 am on Tuesday morning and he still hadn't knocked. She'd tried to sleep, but her mind kept replaying the TV broadcast and her shock had subsided into anger. How could she possibly choose between her family?

Deciding it was impossible to get any more sleep, she crept over to the door. About one hour ago she'd heard voices downstairs but now there was silence.

Her bedroom wasn't actually that bad. There were old oak beams running along the ceiling with musty paintings framed on the walls. While it all seemed quite run down, it was cosy in a homely sort of way.

The bartender had been kind enough to leave a key to the room on her bedside table, so Faye thought it was probably safe to walk around the pub. There wouldn't be many people downstairs, but the 24 hour opening times that applied to every restaurant and public house meant that students stayed out planning for longer. As long as she was careful, she should be okay though.

She slotted the key into the lock and twisted it until she heard it click. Placing the rusty key back on the table, she creaked the door open and peered onto the landing. Faye took about four steps into the corridor when she realized that not only had she left her shoes inside, but also the room key. Knowing she couldn't let the door close; she turned to stop it just as it slammed shut. Now she would have to go downstairs without any shoes on and ask for a spare key.

Prisms

Perfect.

She took the stairs carefully and landed with a soft thud on the pub floor. The door in front of her had a metal sign that said, 'Please Come In' in big bold letters, so she carefully opened and closed it behind her. As she did this, Faye heard movement from upstairs and a few doors shutting.

The bar was deserted apart from the bartender. He sat in front of the bar slumped on one of the tables. There were several pint glasses around him and he appeared to be very drunk. Just don't make too much eye contact and look confident, Faye reassured herself.

She edged nearer to him and could hear him mumbling. "That's karma, gets you for helping a terror-criminal peoples." He hiccupped and stared at the TV screen.

Not quite sure what to say, Faye asked, "Did anyone get hurt?"

The bartender looked around in a daze for a moment, trying to decide whether his mind was playing tricks on him, then realized it was Faye who had spoken. He glared at her for about a minute then bellowed, "You. You should not go here." The words sounded slurred, but Faye was definite about what she'd heard. "Watch that box girl."

Faye was taken aback by his sudden rudeness. Thinking it was probably safer just to watch the TV, she fixed her eyes on the screen.

It was a report about the day's football scores on the news, followed by the week's weather. Faye thought it was absolutely pointless watching, so turned to ask for another key. As she went to speak he ordered, "Watch that!" Faye began to grow impatient but she didn't want to argue with the alcoholic barman.

The same broadcast as earlier came on and then was followed by a brand new news story. A reporter appeared on screen. "In other news, Sponsors released information this morning that could lead to a major breakthrough in tackling illegal Lamplight immigration. Officials have informed news networks that they are looking for a potential terror suspect. Known to be involved in extremist resistance groups, the suspect is wanted immediately for questioning. They have urged us to ask that the public remain ever vigilant and report any sighting of this suspect last seen in the greater London area. We'll update you with any developments on this story as they happen."

Faye stared in horror at the screen. There were no words. It couldn't be right, it was ridiculous. There, right in the middle, was a picture of her with her name under it. She was the suspect wanted for questioning.

Beginning to panic, Faye thought about the lies she'd just heard on the television. She was no terror suspect or extremist resistant member. She was a seventeen year old girl! Surely they'd got it wrong.

"You're a nasty criminal," the bartender accused. "I will not have you, around me in your pub."

Faye thought she understood the general gist of what he was saying. Then, he stood and began to lumber toward her, pointing at her. In response, she took several measured paces backwards. "I've called the Sponsors on you. They get here fifty ... fifteen minutes."

Faye couldn't believe what the man was telling her. Could the Sponsors detain her for something she hadn't done? This was really messed up. She seriously needed help. As she tried to reason what was the next logical thing to do, it dawned on Faye that help might literally be under her very nose. She looked for the pendant round her neck and realized she'd taken it off in her room.

Apparently, all she had to do was stand in the Lamplight and twist it then her father would somehow send her help. At least, that's what Dax had said and she hoped to God he was right. In her current situation, it seemed to Faye as if that was the only plan she had.

Throwing the stair door open, Faye launched herself up the steps and ran down the corridor to her room. The paintings became portraits of people judging her and the corridors felt claustrophobic. It wasn't homely anymore, it was threatening. Damn! she thought. What about the key?

She was about to turn back, when she noticed that there was already a key in her lock. Not pausing to assess how odd this was, she clicked the lock and opened the door. That was her second mistake.

Faye sprinted inside and reached her pendant just as she heard the door close behind her. As she began to turn, she felt two pairs of arms grab her from either side. Taken off guard she lost balance, giving the arms time to throw her to the floor.

Their weight pinned her as she struggled to get free. She felt a cloth over her mouth and someone pressing down hard above her. She tried to scream for help but only muffled noise came out. Her struggling began to slow and the edges of Faye's vision went blurry. Her legs lost their kicking momentum and became still. Trying to fight the growing sensation of tiredness, Faye realized too late it was chloroform. Who the hell would want to drug her! Her eyes closed, just as a man's face framed by magenta hair came into view.

* * *

Faye began to wake but could only see snapshots of where she was. She felt woozy and couldn't exactly remember what had happened; just that it wasn't really part of her plan. Faye wanted to get up and find out where she was, but her eyes wouldn't comply.

She could see lights above her. Fairy lights? And were there leaves too? Closing her eyes again she decided she must be delusional. A few hours of sleep couldn't hurt.

* * *

Someone was putting water to her lips. It helped at first, but gushed down her throat too fast. Faye tried to sit up. She felt a light pressure on her forehead, forcing her to remain lying down.

There was a shadow blocking out the light and she heard a man's voice say, "Easy, easy now. It'll take some time for it to be out of your system completely." He sounded quite young but there was a hard edge to his voice. The kind of tone you'd expect from a soldier. Faye swore she recognized his voice from somewhere.

She reached one of her hands to her head and tried to rub the sleep away from her eyes. Slowly she opened them and was forced to squint against the light.

"Get the lights Dave; she's starting to wake up." Suddenly the bright light was gone, and she could see spots of light instead. Like tiny dots or stars in the ceiling.

"Help me up," Faye croaked. Her voice sounded hoarse and her throat felt dry. A strong hand grabbed her arm while another supported her back as Faye began to sit up. Her head spun, she felt extremely dizzy and her back ached from lying on what felt like a wooden table.

The voice again said, "It will take some time to adjust. I'll explain everything when you're properly awake."

Faye's vision was starting to return and she could make out her surroundings now. It appeared to be another pub, but very different to the last one. There were small tables nestled into little cubby holes, with a larger one underneath her. Gold twigs and leaves covered the surface of the low ceiling and fairy lights hung among them and around the room. Candles lit the tables, and she noticed a chalk board next to her. She could see scratches and scuffs where it had been abused for many years by the board rubber, and small multi colored shards of chalk had fallen onto the wall edge below. On one wall, there was a flag printed with the words 'Power to the Resistance'.

"The flag," Faye croaked. She turned to look at the man who was still supporting her and said, "I think I know you."

He stared at her with silver eyes. "I'm a friend of Dax. I've met you a couple of times before. He said you'd come here after he left you, but you didn't show. We came and found you instead."

Faye looked completely confused. "You've seen Dax?" Faye asked. "Can I see him?"

The man looked at the flag and said, "He's gone away for a while but I promise that now you have our protection. He was a very active member of the resistance and besides, we can't have a wanted criminal walking round the streets now can we?" He smiled at her, revealing his youth. If he was a friend of Dax, he must be about the same age as him.

Still perplexed by what was going on, Faye remembered. "Hey, you attacked me!" She attempted to hit him, but he moved swiftly out the way. She coughed as the remnants of whatever she'd been given lingered in her lungs. "That's not exactly very good protection is it!"

The man considered this. "The Sponsors knew you were inside and we had to get you out of the pub without anyone in it being aware you were leaving. If we'd asked you to leave with us, you would've screamed."

Faye thought about what he'd said and begrudgingly answered, "Okay, fair point. That's probably true."

The man ran his hands through his magenta hair. "I'm Mat, by the way. You're completely safe here with us. Oh, and we've got your things for you."

Faye looked grateful. "Thanks Mat." She reached for her pendant and felt it wasn't there. "Or maybe I shouldn't be too thankful just yet ..."

Mat noticed her doing this and said, "Ah, and we've got your pendant too. But before we give it to you, I think we seriously need to talk."

Chapter 11
The Missing Link

2.00 am, Tuesday morning, five days left until the Runners came and Kash was in the middle of breaking into a house. She'd seen the news broadcast and the wanted notice for Dax's sister. This meant her job of finding Faye had just been made one thousand times harder. What on Mara had she got herself mixed up in!

On leaving 'Simms and Sons', she'd walked around trying to find inspiration and when she'd given up, Kash had sat in a restaurant for quite some time, sipping dry Martini on the rocks. Kash knew her best bet of finding some way to reach Faye was in Centar, so after a rather unproductive afternoon, she'd rented a room in a nearby hotel. She hadn't accounted for how much a hotel in the capital would cost.

Before all this, Kash would've sworn that she knew Dax inside out, but now she wasn't so sure. How many other secrets had he kept from her?

This had made her think. Secrets that no one else would know, but the one secret he'd entrusted to her.

Dax had a cover job selling stationery, but that wasn't his main job. Kash cursed her stupidity for not thinking of it earlier. Sitting in the hotel room she'd thought, Of course! The patches!

It was odd, but Kash thought she'd never been so happy about her fiancé's illegal trading habits. He sold patches to Marans so they could go to earth. She'd never even considered trying them before because it was against the law, but now it seemed she had no alternative. The one tiny flaw in her brilliant plan was that she didn't have a clue what Dax had done with them. If he'd taken them to London she could stop searching now, but it would be pointless to do that so she thought it unlikely. She was absolutely positive they weren't in her house in Hem, because if they were she would have murdered Dax by now. Taking this into account, Kash thought that the most likely place where the patches could be stored was in Dax's own house.

Although Kash had never actually broken into a house before, she wasn't stupid enough to try it in the daylight. It was kind of exciting though, sneaking out and trying to evade the Sponsors. Kash wore all black, with a baseball cap to cover her hair and sunglasses to tint her bright eyes. It was only after Kash had put the glasses on that she realized it was impossible to see anything when it was dark outside.

Keeping to the shadows, Kash had crept around Centar in the very early hours of the morning, narrowly missing two patrolling Sponsors. She'd been doing really well until she'd walked into a wall and shouted, "OW!"

Kash was forced to run the remainder of her journey. When she'd reached the Link house, she'd forgotten how beautiful it was.

Largely, the house was brown and white with an artificial yet very convincing lawn out the front. There was a password sensitive lock on the iron gates that stopped people from entering the house and a very high wall that ran round the perimeter. It was one of the perks you got for being an executive, well-paid member of the conference. The house was practically a miniature mansion.

But this was a big downfall for Kash. Not only would there be hundreds of potential places she could look, but that would be obsolete if she couldn't even get past the gate. There was no keypad because it was a well-known fact that they could be easily guessed or hacked. Kash thought this was ridiculous, but it seemed more likely that now she would have more chance of succeeding if it was a keypad.

Kash wasn't the quietest of people either, so she'd be lucky to even make it onto the grass undetected. After she'd moved closer to the gate, an electronic panel had appeared. A robotic automated voice said, "Five guesses remaining." Fantastic, she thought. If guessing a password wasn't hard enough I've only got five attempts to get it!

It was vital that she got inside the house so Kash really needed to open the gate. In the past she'd never needed the password, Dax or someone else had always let her in. If she could just remember what Dax had said last time, she could open it.

Think Kash think! she thought angrily to herself. Now what did Dax say last time?

She tried to recall their last conversation, but her terrible short term memory was making it really difficult for her. That's it, she thought.

* * *

"Dax, I bought you that jacket to wear, not to use as a shield from the rain," Kash joked. She was absolutely drenched from the sudden storm and raindrops were still falling around her. "If you don't open this gate soon, I'm going to drown."

Dax smiled wryly at her and placed the jacket through a gap in the gate. "You know," he said, taking a piece of her soaking hair between his fingers, "you look so sexy when it's raining."

Kash glared at him. "It's no use trying to get on my good side, I'm soaked through. Please, just open the gate."

Dax kissed her on the cheek and said—

* * *

Said what? Kash thought. Stupid, STUPID short term memory! She couldn't remember what Dax had said next and it would probably have been the password. It was hopeless, she needed to get inside. Then, Kash had a brainwave. It was probably ridiculous but it was the best she had at the moment. Perhaps it was his name that unlocked the gate.

She leant toward the panel and whispered into it. "Dax Link." She looked furtively around her to make sure no one was watching and then saw the panel count from four to five; one guess down.

Rethinking her guess, she decided it would be sensible to try Faye's full name since she didn't know Dax's. That was bad, her own fiancé and she didn't even know his middle name! Kash faced the panel again and said, "Anna Faye Link." Nothing happened for a moment then the panel flashed from four to three. Kash didn't stand a chance if she kept guessing randomly like this. Who would use their name as a password anyway?

Beginning to panic, she tried desperately to recall the rest of their conversation. Snippets of it started coming back to her and she began to remember more.

* * *

"Okay, but I do mean it. Oh, before we go in, I should probably tell you something."

Kash looked at him. "Is it 'I can't wait to open this gate and get out of the rain'?"

Dax grinned and replied, "No, you weren't even close. I'm planning to tell dad today that we're going to buy a house together."

Kash's face lightened. "You are? Today?"

Dax nodded. "Yeah. I think we're ready to let him know. And anyway, I want you to properly get to know your family in law." Dax had never really been that family orientated and hadn't talked to his sister in about a year, so he had quite a bit of catching up to do.

"That's sweet honey, but I'm still soaking."

Dax laughed and—

* * *

And what? Kash accused her memory. There had been no clues that she could use and in that conversation the gate was still closed.

In annoyance, Kash shouted, "Why won't you open you stupid gate?" She got even angrier when the counter flashed from three to two.

Considering that shouting is probably the quickest way to get caught; she cupped a hand over her own mouth and looked around to see if anyone had noticed. No one was running toward her or raising alarms, so Kash decided she was probably safe to keep trying.

She closed her eyes and calmed herself down. Then, leaning into the panel again, she said, "Hi there, I'm Faye and I've forgotten the password. Can you just let me in please?" Needless to say, the panel counted from two to one and observed, "You have one guess remaining."

This was so frustrating, why couldn't their father just open the gate! As she lingered on this thought, she noticed that she'd never actually been told Mr. Link's first name. Or, perhaps she had been told and it hadn't properly registered.

* * *

Dax finally agreed. "Fine, I'll open it."

Kash hugged her fiancé. "Thanks, I might need to borrow a hair dryer and some spare clothes though," she joked.

Dax laughed. "No Problem."

Just as he leant toward the gate, Kash asked, "Do you think your father will like me?"

He turned to Kash. "Without a shadow of a doubt, my father Frazer James Link will love you." Dax stepped through the gate and took Kash's hand as they walked toward the house.

* * *

Kash thought that had to be it.

Leaning one last time toward the panel, she spoke clearly. "Frazer James Link."

Nothing happened for a while then the counter flashed from one to zero. Expecting an alarm, Kash began to sprint away from the gate, just as it opened.

She turned in shock, stretched and said out loud, "I knew it was going to do that!" Kash stepped through the gate thinking that no one would be able to spot her. This, however, was not true. As she began to walk down the long drive, floodlights suddenly bathed the area in brilliant white light, leaving not one shadow untouched.

For a couple of minutes Kash stood still, like a rabbit caught in headlights then she ran toward the house. As she did this, sprinklers switched on spraying the grass and herself. By the time she reached the front door, she'd managed to leave the gate wide open, alert the whole neighborhood she was breaking into the house, turn on ridiculously powerful floodlights and soak herself by switching on the sprinklers. Kash decided that she was officially the worst burglar in the history of the world.

Prisms

Standing on the porch, she thought it would be too easy to just walk through the door. As she went to find another entrance, perhaps like a window, the door said, "Welcome to the Link residence Ms. Trix." It was more a speaking panel in the door than the door itself, but it was still a bit freaky. Kash was even more surprised when the same door opened. Obviously there was a face detection camera somewhere, or voice recognition, or something like that. "Shame you couldn't open the gate for me then!"

So, it was 2.00 am on Tuesday morning, five days left until the Runners came and Kash was in the middle of breaking into a house. Well, she reasoned it wasn't really breaking in if the house seemed to know your name.

Kash stepped into the large hallway and all the lights in the house appeared to turn on. She shut the door behind her and took a moment to marvel at the beauty of the room. A winding iron staircase stretched up two floors, and the wooden floor shone from the polish. There were several white corner sofas and a large stainless coffee table, with modern works of art dotted around the room. She decided it was more of a reception room than a hallway, but whatever it was Kash didn't have time to admire it. She had to find the patches.

Thinking to herself, where would I hide illegal goods from my family? Kash decided the most obvious place would be in her own bedroom. No one would check there because it was so obvious. This was based purely on theory but it seemed to be the only idea Kash had, so she went with it.

She climbed the iron stairs to the second floor where she knew Dax's bedroom was and stopped to think. It was a reasonable sized room with a lot of clutter. There were a couple of desks covered with papers and photos, with several cardboard boxes around the room. His bed took up much of the space and the blue and white walls made it feel much bigger than it actually was. A wide screen cube sat in one corner of the room and a treadmill took up the remainder of the space.

Kash discounted the en-suite bathroom for the time being and began to search the cardboard boxes. Kash and her fiancé were remarkably similar, so she reasoned that it made sense they'd be on largely the same wavelength. Many, contained packets of pens, rulers and rubbers, but some contained stickers. The types of stickers children might use to decorate anything and everything.

Kash opened up one of the packets and sure enough between the sheets, were small neck patches. Maybe she'd found them so quickly because she knew Dax so well, or perhaps he was just an idiot for not hiding them well enough. She'd ask him when she found him.

Not wanting to wait around in case Sponsors showed up and arrested her for breaking and entering, Kash grabbed about ten packets and dashed out of the bedroom. She virtually flew down the staircase and ran to the front door.

Kash threw the door open and found she was face to face with a man she knew. A man she'd not seen in a rather long time. He looked at her puzzled, crossed his arms and saw the packets of stickers in her hands.

"Hi, Mr. Link," she said.

Chapter 12
How to Snap A Caine

It was a comfortable life being leader of the world, but there had always been a thorn in Torre Fynn's side. A thorn that as it currently stood, he could not pull out. This annoyance was Jonathon Caine. Fynn couldn't see the need for two worldly leaders. It was a conflict of interests and neither leader could ever agree with the other. Caine had to go. Besides, Fynn was a public persona, whereas Caine was unfit to even give a speech to the nation. Today, Fynn was going to destroy Caine.

He sat at the head of the long ebony conference table, facing the man he wanted to crush. Executives lined the two sides, hiding behind clipboards and notebooks. None of them had any real spine and they didn't deserve positions of such power. They were pawns in Fynn's game and he was one move away from winning.

It was 12.00pm on Tuesday and Fynn was counting the days until his elite force took control. Fynn leant forward in his grand leather chair and surveyed the room.

"Good afternoon," he addressed the conference. Every pair of eyes round the table snapped to look at him and silence descended upon the room. "I have called this meeting in reference to my latest commitment to the Runner program. I believe they are essential to the development of society and the two worlds will be closer for it."

Caine stood up and slammed his hand down on the table. "That is ridiculous," he accused pointing at Fynn, "and worse still, you know it is." Caine took a step back. "Who here feels the need for change in our system?"

He was fighting a battle he was bound to lose. Every hand in the room was raised and Fynn sat smug in his chair.

"This is an outrage!" roared Caine. "Mr. Fynn, pray tell us what you hope to accomplish by isolating both worlds consecutively."

Matching his opponent, Fynn stood and again spoke to the listening executives. "We will eradicate the majority of crime by improving the communication between the worlds. It is hardly isolation if contact is organized and audited through the conference.

"The black market trade will decrease by 60%. Resistance groups will begin to disband. Everything I hope to accomplish will bring about worldly peace, not prevent it. There will be no racial hatred. Everything will be for the better." Feeling confident in his argument, Fynn sat back down and folded his arms.

His temper rising, Caine demanded, "How can you predict such ludicrous claims. If anything, the resistance figures will double! The Runners are a worldwide threat, not an ally."

Fynn looked completely relaxed and mildly amused, as if Caine was a screaming child and this was just another tantrum. He stroked his manicured silver beard once and clasped both hands calmly in front of him.

Tackling it from another angle, Caine asked, "You're a family man Torre. How would you feel if your beloved daughter Clare was removed? How would it feel to know that you had sealed her fate and sent her to the same grave as her mother?"

The executives shuffled nervously in their seats and sat in complete silence. It was a dangerous move to involve personal life in conference affairs and Caine had just pole vaulted over the line.

Fynn's face was cold and his eyes were smoldering. He tried not to reveal his emotions, but for the first time in his life, Fynn was vulnerable and exposed to Caine's attack.

Fynn stood and glared at Caine in rage and disbelief. He looked so menacing that even the room guards subconsciously took a step back. Fynn leant forward over the desk and spat, "My personal affairs should be of no matter of consequence to the conference. I put the needs of both worlds first and right now what they need is order, an order I am going to give to them. A single sacrifice is for the good of thousands and I intend to maintain this belief when the Runners come."

Fynn stepped away from his chair and began to walk slowly

past the cowering executives toward Caine. As he did this, he continued to speak through clenched teeth. "I am the greater power. I control who succeeds and who fails, and I have the right to change both mine and your world for the better. No one will challenge this, because if they do, I will strike such a blow that I will most definitely crush them. Years of work and time dedicated to the conference will become absolutely obsolete, and do you know why?"

Caine stared at the man who now stood next to him and looked into the eyes that were now inches away from his own.

"BECAUSE I, AM, THE GREATER, POWER!" Fynn shouted. There were a few moments of complete silence as the room was stunned by this revelation. No one had the courage to stand up to this tyrant; no one had the power to speak out against him.

Caine walked backwards as Fynn used his chair to stand on the table. He enjoyed the look of terror in the eyes of those present in the room. How pathetic. He began to pace up and down the length of ebony, then stopped halfway. "This is how it shall be." Fynn commanded. "No one will question the Runner program, NO ONE," he bellowed. "I need to know that the conference is in full support of the program and I owe it to you all to identify the chink in our chain mail. The weakest link, so to speak. It is my duty to eradicate the one plagued person who will compromise our entire campaign; our entire future."

Fynn looked seriously around the room then straightened himself and pointed directly at Caine. "There, is such a person. Jonathon Caine will RUIN the entire operation and we cannot have someone compromise such an important program.

"There is only need for one leader. One leader to unite both worlds; one leader to propel us further into the future and that leader, is ME."

Caine looked as if he was about to challenge this, then thought it safer not to.

With no objection Fynn continued, "All those in favor of me rising as a single worldly leader." Every executive raised a tentative hand and every room guard saluted.

"You cowards!" Caine spat.

"May I take this moment to thank the conference in their just choice of leader. It is an honor to have the opportunity to structure such a well-oiled team of people."

As Fynn was still standing on the table as he said this, it looked like he was accepting some sort of award on stage. Then, his face fell grave and he looked toward Caine with accusing eyes. "As your new leader, I feel it necessary to enforce my first conviction."

Caine's face dropped as he realized what Fynn was about to do. "Fynn, think very carefully before you do this," he warned, but Fynn's mind was already made up.

"Jonathan Caine ..." Fynn announced.

"Fynn, think what you're doing here," Caine interrupted.

"I convict you of treason against the conference, conspiring, and involvement in acts of terrorism. The punishment of which currently stands at permanent removal. I hereby pass this conviction and act as judge, jury and executioner when I state that Jonathon Caine, you are found GUILTY."

Fynn had won. He'd managed to obliterate the one person who stood between himself and total power, and now he could even control who lived and who died.

The guards rushed forth and seized Caine by either arm. "Please Torre, I beg you to show mercy, I have two daughters waiting for their daddy to come home." Caine spoke hurriedly. "I have a wife who lies dying in hospital from a terminal illness, who I need to tend to daily. Please, I urge you to reconsider; I will do anything to see them again."

Whether this was a pathetic last ditch attempt to save his life and incite pity or not, Fynn didn't care. He didn't cave into pleas for mercy. Fynn strode down the table toward him and jumped to the floor. Then he laid his blazer beside him and said, "I'm sorry Jonathon, but we shouldn't let our personal affairs interfere in the conference. It's the first rule of business."

The guards dragged the hysterical man from the room and slammed the large oak door behind. There was one final scream followed by a flash of light that was visible through the cracks in the door. Then total silence descended upon the room.

Fynn smiled, and turned slowly to face the conference. "Any questions?" he asked.

Chapter 13
The Perfect Weapon

Mat had allowed Faye to get some sleep by showing her to his own bedroom. The place was more like a network of rooms, or a secret complex than a pub. Mat's room was fairly small and cramped, with old newspaper cuttings lining the walls. He had a pin board with things like old tickets and photos stuck to it and apart from his bed there was a wardrobe, but that was it. Quite characterful, Faye had thought, but a shame about the lack of books.

Surprisingly, Faye had managed to get a good eight hours sleep. Safe in the knowledge she was protected by friends of Dax, it had been easier to drift off. Now, the time was 11pm on Tuesday and Faye was ready to talk properly with the students.

Mat had said when she was ready to see him again she should ring an old bell that appeared to be attached to some sort of wire. It hung precariously from the top shelf and rust formed around the base of the bell. Not sure about what it would do, she reached up cautiously and tugged the rope that hung from it. Because it was such an old pub she could hear footsteps above her racing down the stairs. Within minutes, her door was open and Mat was standing before her.

"Want to meet the team?" He grinned.

Faye laughed. "Maybe, but I'm not fantastic with names. I think just keep it to the people who are essential."

"Fair enough." Mat shrugged, and motioned for her to follow him.

They climbed down the steep uneven set of stairs at the end of the seemingly endless corridor and entered the same room that Faye had originally woken up in. There was just one other person waiting for them in the bar, and on their arrival he stood up and uncrossed his arms, folding them behind his back. On the table beside him was a funny looking machine with numerous wires coming off it and some sort of gauge.

When Mat and Faye reached him, he stretched out a hand toward her and said, "I'm David Pringle, nice to meet you." This guy sounded even more like a soldier than Mat and his broad shoulders confirmed this.

Faye giggled and asked, "Like, the crisp?"

David looked at her sheepishly then answered, "No, not really."

"Sorry," Faye said, now looking just as embarrassed. Why did I just make such a fool of myself? she questioned.

Moving swiftly on, David continued, "I see you've met my partner, Mat Coyne."

Faye stared at him. "Oh, you're both gay?"

Both men laughed.

"Cheers Dave. No, he means partners in crime, in the resistance, that sort of thing," Mat said.

"Oh, sorry," she apologized again.

David's lips formed into a hard line and he shifted uncomfortably from one foot to the other. Mat gestured for her to sit in the chair next to the machine. Now, the friendly kidnappers were much more intimidating.

As she sat down, Mat ordered, "Okay, you need to sit still now. We're going to ask you a few questions, but first we're going to connect you to this machine. We will attach the set of wires to your left hand and you'll hold the metal rod in your right. Do you understand?"

Faye nodded and didn't say anything. She wasn't an expert on how procedures went in these situations, but she was pretty sure this wasn't normal.

It took about twenty minutes to configure the machine and attach all the wires before Mat and David were ready to start.

David looked very obviously human with short brown hair and brown eyes. He had a fairly muscular build and wore a T-shirt and pair of combat shorts. Clearly he hadn't realized they were into the coldest season of the year.

Prisms

Mat flicked a switch on the side of the machine and announced, "Right, we're ready to begin. David will ask you a few standard questions first, answer with a yes or a no."

* * *

"Is your name Anna Faye Link."
    "Yes."
    "Are you 17 years old?"
    "Yes."
    "Do you have a brother called Dax?"
    "Yes."
    "Do you or Dax work for the conference?"
    "No."
    "Have either of you worked for the conference in the past."
    "No."
    "Do you know the whereabouts of your father?"
    "... No"
    "Are the allegations relating to you on the news true?"
    "No!"
    "Do you know the true function of your pendant?"
    "No, well I do kinda but ... oh, sorry, no."
    "Have any other resistance groups contacted you?"
    "No."
    "Are you wearing a tracker that could allow people to follow you or pinpoint your location?"
    "No."

* * *

Mat flicked the machine off. "She told the truth every time," he said.
    "Is that a lie detector?" Faye asked.
Mat began to unattach the wires. "Yes, but only because you can never be too sure these days. It was necessary."
It was 12:20pm when the machine had been completely disconnected and another student had run into the room demanding that they watch the news. It seemed like watching the news was a social event in these resistances.
All three people followed the student into a large crowded space

and gathered round to watch the TV. On screen there was an image of Jonathon Caine with the words 'Breaking News' printed in bold beneath it.

A reporter read, "Good afternoon. We interrupt your broadcast to bring you breaking news from the conference. Torre Fynn has been made the acting worldly leader following the removal of Jonathon Caine. Sponsors have released information that terrorist Anna Link and a group of accomplices are responsible and believe she acquired removal technology from an unknown source. We have been informed that she used this technology when Caine was on a residential visit to London."

On the screen was a picture of her and five other people. An artist's impression of non-descript faceless people, who really could have been anyone. The only identifiable picture was Faye's and it was obvious who was being accused. Then, another image appeared on screen. Underneath it read 'Clare Fynn'.

"Sponsors also have reason to believe that the daughter of worldly leader Torre Fynn was involved in the plot to remove Jonathon Caine and a warrant has similarly been issued for her immediate detention. We now go live to the Lamplight to bring you Torre Fynn's reaction."

Fynn appeared on screen behind a bank of microphones on a raised platform. There were hundreds of flashing cameras and television crews reporting on the story.

Fynn began to speak. "On the brink of change and a new era of control, it is a tragedy that such a great leader has fallen. The brutal actions of Anna Link and the involvement of Clare Fynn will not go unpunished. The Sponsors will not rest until they are found and brought to justice. That is all I have to say on the matter."

Fynn began to step down off the platform as the camera man asked, "Mr. Fynn, what implications will there be due to the relation between yourself and one of the accused?"

Fynn stared straight at the camera. "No comment."

Faye was again stunned into silence. She'd been in the middle of a lie detector test when she'd apparently removed Caine. The students around Faye stared at her in awe and all began to cheer and clap. They were hugging her and congratulating her on the success.

Faye was visibly uncomfortable and upset with this news, so Mat and David acted as body guards to escort her out of the room.

84

Prisms

They supported her into the bar again, made her sit down and got her a glass of water.

"I ... I was ... here," Faye stuttered.

Noticing she was in shock, Mat said, "We know it wasn't you. We know everything they've said has been a lie and we won't rest until Fynn is held to account for it."

Faye couldn't even nod. She just sat there trying to make sense of what had happened. She was dragged sharply back to reality when David slapped her.

"What in the worlds did you do that for?!" Faye shouted.

David looked at Mat and shrugged. "You were hysterical?"

"No I wasn't!" she continued to holler, "You slap like a girl!"

"Can you please stop shouting!" Mat bellowed. "Thank you."

Faye glared at him, but he continued anyway, "Faye, this is perfect. They might be looking for you, but they won't find you. And your pendant? It's extremely rare; no wonder they want you found immediately. If the public was to truly see what went on in the conference, there would be riots in the streets."

"Right, now I'm just confused," Faye admitted.

"Your pendant allows the user to enter the Lamplight. If you twist it when standing in the light, you can get inside the conference and show the world what really goes on. Faye, you have the chance to destroy Torre Fynn before he destroys you."

Faye considered this for a moment. "I'm not entirely happy about destroying someone, I don't do this kind of stuff. I'm not even legal to drink yet!"

David looked away uninterestedly and went back to standing at ease.

The lights in the ceiling flickered as a heavy thud pounded on the floorboards above. "Right, well I guess in the given situation I don't have much choice then, do I."

Mat gazed at her with hopeful eyes. "Not really, no. You are the perfect weapon. All the guards will be on Earth looking for you, so you can access the Lamplight undetected. We'll help you prepare and we'll keep in contact with you at all times. What do you say?"

Both Mat and David waited expectantly.

It was tense for a moment in the room then Faye made up her mind. "Fine I'm in. When do I start?" she announced.

Chapter 14
Finding Faye

It was so like Torre to pull a stunt like this, Clare thought. No one else would have the audacity to put a wanted picture on the news of his own daughter. It made her blood boil just thinking about him. He knew what her plan would be. He would've known before she'd figured out what the plan was.

Breaking out of the complex had actually been pretty simple. It was less like a mad dash for the exit and more like a leisurely stroll to the door. After Lark had persuaded Clare to come with him, he'd simply used his new finger print ID to open all the doors on the way to the ground floor of the tower.

Several guards asked Lark what he was doing and he'd replied, "I'm escorting the girl back to Mara on Mr. Fynn's orders." They'd nodded and waved him on. Stupid security system, Clare could've evaded them in her sleep.

However, they did come across one problem at reception. When he'd explained where he was taking Clare, the guard hadn't believed him. As the guard had begun to pick up the phone to clarify if this was correct, Lark had gone and stood next to him. Then with a hand on his shoulder, Lark had squeezed it very slightly, rendering the man unconscious. It wasn't the most ethical of methods, but it got the job done. Clare wouldn't admit that she was ever so slightly impressed.

As soon as Lark and Clare were in the light, he'd grabbed her arm and they were suddenly in Covent Garden. There wasn't even as much as a jolt; it had been as natural as walking through an open door.

Lark was amazed. This was his first time on another world and the enormity of his job was beginning to sink in. Without wearing a patch, his Maran colors were not neutralized and he stuck out in the crowd like a sore thumb. The sun reflected off his pure white hair, causing passersby to stop and stare. Everything seemed just a bit dull in comparison to Mara. All the colors were boring and no one seemed to be in a rush to go anywhere. For a new world, it was kind of disappointing.

"Welcome to Earth," Clare said. Then she tried unsuccessfully to make a run for it. Lark still had a tight grip on her arm that made it impossible to leave.

"Are you going to be as protective the whole trip?" she asked.

Lark laughed. "Think of it less like protection and more like detention."

"Oh yeah, 'cause that sounds so much better," Clare snapped sarcastically. "And why are we in Covent Garden?"

Lark took one last look around at his new surroundings. "This is Faye's last know location. We need to find a local resistance group and ask them for information."

Clare snorted. "What makes you think they'll trust you enough to give you information?"

A wide grin spread across Lark's face. It was the type of grin that would've looked quite disturbing in the dark. "Well, now that I'm traveling with someone wanted for involvement in the resistance and someone wanted for the removal of Jonathon Caine, they'll welcome us with open arms."

"This was all part of your plan wasn't it?" Clare asked surprised.

"Don't act so shocked darling, surely you and your intellect figured that out before you agreed to come and help me?" Lark waited for a response but didn't get one. "Aww, poor Clare played right into mine and daddy's hands. You know, he's very clever like that. Either way it's a win-win situation for me or rather, a catch 22 for you; poor naïve Clare."

Clare didn't understand how she could've missed this. Why hadn't she figured this out before? She'd had the best part of the morning to work it out and now it was 10.00am. It was okay though because there was one plan, besides her plan to escape, that her father wouldn't be aware of.

"Now, we can't stand here all day so where on Earth are the most likely resistance gatherings?"

Clare glared at him with angry eyes.

"Clare, sooner or later you're going to help me because if you don't, you'll be seeing the inside of a cell again sooner than you think."

Grinding her teeth together, Clare spat, "In the pubs."

"Brilliant," Lark beamed. "We'll go find the nearest pub."

Clare hated him. Lark was a hypocrite and a cunning idiot. Not too long ago he'd been committed to his own resistance and he'd vowed never to change his ideals, but now? Now he was spearheading the greatest cover up operation in Maran history. She found it hard to see how someone could change so dramatically over such a short period of time. Oh what power does to a man.

What Lark didn't realize, was that taking Clare to meet Faye was a bad idea. Clare decided that when they found Faye, she'd warn her about who Lark really was and then turn the whole resistance on him. They were bound to back her and Faye if they thought they were big players in the resistance. It would be all too easy to isolate Lark. The only flaw in her once again amazing plan was that for it to work, she'd have to be alone with Faye to tell her. If Lark was around, she'd be sent to the complex before she could even get her words out. Right now it was the best plan she had, so she'd help him find Faye and then ruin him. It was foolproof. She so badly wanted to boast about it to Lark. See, I'm not just a pretty face, Clare would spit at him.

Clare and Lark had walked round Covent Garden for about five minutes before they found a pub. Clare would help him find the elusive Anna, but she'd have her fun first. He wanted to hold her captive? Well, then that would be his problem.

They pushed open the pub door and stepped into an empty bar. An old bartender sat behind the worn wood looking vacantly into the distance.

"Where is everyone?" hissed Lark.

Clare attempted to look innocent. "I don't know."

Lark would have totally believed her if she wasn't trying so hard to be aloof.

"Clare do not toy with me, if they're not here then, Where. Are. They?"

It was so frustrating that she'd have to tell him eventually. "Fine. They don't meet until night."

"And that's all you need to tell me?" Lark questioned.

Clare thought it was safer just to nod this time, but he still saw straight through her.

Lark swung one of the bar stools round to face Clare and used it to pin her against the wall behind. "Seriously, don't test me girl. I am this close to removing you myself."

She'd never felt it before with him, but now she was terrified of the rage in his eyes and the malice in his voice. There went her plan to have some fun. "They wouldn't meet in a public place. They tend to gather in pubs down dark alleyways, or off the tourist trail. You'd be lucky to find any resistance members in pubs off the main square."

Lark's eyes bore into her for a moment, then he assessed she was telling the truth. "You could've saved so much hassle by telling me that the first time round. Don't try it again," Lark cautioned, punching her playfully on the arm. "If they only meet at night, we've got some time to kill; fancy going to the opera?"

* * *

Tuesday was now officially the worst day of the week. She'd spent the day with Lark pretending to bond over opera, going shopping in the shops that were still open and acting like she'd enjoyed his company over dinner. Now the time was 8.00pm, the perfect time for a pub gathering.

Clare and Lark were en route to a well-known resistance haunt called 'The Barrel and Barman'. It was famous on the wire for being packed to the roof with passionate young students with dreams of change. It was dark enough outside to slip along the streets largely unnoticed, but early enough not to be caught by Sponsors.

Eventually, they reached the pub and Lark gestured for Clare to enter it first. When they got inside, they were given the biggest surprise of their lives. There were no students sat among the tables. Instead, four Sponsors were questioning the bartender. This was Faye's last known location alright. One of the men held a poster with Faye's and Clare's face on it but before she had the chance to leave, Lark walked in behind her and managed to grab the attention of the Sponsors by ringing the bell above the door.

One of the men took a quick step forward holding a clipper, while the other three men produced guns. Taken aback by the guards' presence, Lark leapt in front of Clare and pulled his own gun. He gripped her arm with his other hand behind him so she couldn't escape.

"Good evening gentlemen," Lark said. "This girl is in my custody. I'm going to put down my gun and reach into my pocket to show you my badge. Let's not be too hasty here."

The men surveyed Lark then the man out front passed the clipper behind him to another Sponsor.

"Why didn't you tell me you had a gun?!" Clare hissed.

Lark snapped back at her. "Now is not the time Clare!" He reached into his pocket and produced a leather badge the size of a business card, which was embossed with the same pattern as on the side of his neck.

"You're a Runner?" questioned one of the Sponsors.

Unsure whether this was a friendly question or not, Lark picked his gun back up and pointed it at the man in front of him. "Yes," he answered, removing the safety catch.

The Sponsor smiled and placed the badge back in Lark's pocket with a gun still aimed at his head. "Correct me if I'm wrong, which I'm not, but don't the Runners start next Monday?" The man grinned, reached behind for the clipper, and held it in front of him. If he reached Clare, she'd be unable to run.

"What's your point?" Lark offered warily.

"Well, it seems that you do not have the authorization to hold this girl in your custody, until Monday. You need to relinquish her to the custody of the Sponsors. Put down the gun and step away from her."

Clare was torn between being scared and being grateful that she might not have to spend another moment with Lark.

"Fine," Lark said, "I guess you're right." He began to lower his gun then quickly pulled Clare in front of him and held the gun to her head.

"Lark, what the hell are you doing?" she said, panic rising in her voice.

"You come one step closer and I kill the girl," Lark warned.

Clare shook her head and said, "I think that's a very bad idea, how about we don't kill the girl."

The front Sponsor took a step back. "Fine, you'll make our job a lot easier."

Lark grimaced and his finger twitched in the trigger.

"Stop!" one of the Sponsors ordered. "We cannot kill Torre Fynn's daughter, it is not our objective."

Lark looked at the speaking Sponsor and demanded, "Well, then this is what's going to happen. I am going to walk out of this pub with the girl and you will not make any attempt to stop me or follow me. If anyone does I will kill her, understood?"

The Sponsors stood silent in front of him and said nothing.

"Is that understood?" Lark shouted. One of the men nodded and began to lower his gun. All the other Sponsors followed suit until all the weapons were on the floor.

Lark began to back out of the door with the gun still pressed to Clare's head. Just before he left, he shouted to the barman, "I am never recommending your pub to any of my friends."

Lark replaced the safety catch and dragged the stunned Clare through the door until they were again standing on the pavement with the Sponsors safely inside.

Clare looked shell shocked. "I'm ... confused. Are you good or ... bad?" she stuttered.

Lark lowered the gun. "Does it matter, just run!"

Chapter 15
Lost in London

Kash had never given much thought to what would happen to her if she was caught breaking into a house, mainly because she hadn't considered burglary as a career path. But now she had been caught red-handed by the one person she looked up to most. Because Kash didn't have a father, she'd always thought of Mr. Link as a father figure and she'd even asked him to give her away at the wedding. So why did such a respected man look so guilty going into his own house? It was more like Kash had caught him breaking in, instead of the other way round.

"Mr. Link, I'm so sorry, I can explain but it will sound weird if I do," Kash stammered. Link looked confused and troubled. Perhaps he was considering how having a criminal daughter in law would affect his family.

Link pushed Kash back inside the house making her trip over her feet, then slammed the door behind. There was urgency in the way his eyes scanned over her and he stared at her with an emotionless expression on his face.

"Kash, I need you to listen carefully to me," Link rushed. "Can you do that and be quiet for a few minutes?"

She had a terrible habit of constantly interrupting people and she could very rarely remain silent. Instead of prolonging the conversation, she just nodded.

"Good. It is imperative that you do not tell anyone that you've seen me. You need to find Faye. She's with a trusted resistance group in London and is staying at 'Birdcage Inn'. The patches you've taken ..."

"Oh yeah, sorry about that," interrupted Kash. Link stared at her waiting for her to finish, then she said, "I'm sorry for interrupting too, please carry on."

Link took a moment to regain his train of thought then continued, "The patches you have will allow you to travel through the Lamplight. Use the streetlamp outside our house; it will not be monitored. Do this around 9.00pm this evening. You may spend the day in our house but you must leave at that time. If you see my son or daughter ..." he faltered for a second, "... tell them ... I love them very much and it will all be over soon, but do not tell them where you met me. Kash, if you tell them any other information about our meeting, it will most certainly place them in danger. Do you understand everything I've told you?"

Kash thought about this. "Kind of, I have a couple of questions though. If you work for the conference then why are you running? And why would they be in danger?!"

Link placed a hand on her shoulder then disappeared up the spiral stairs.

"Hello! That's not an answer!" Kash shouted after him. Well, at least the house was big enough not to get bored in. There was a room stacked high with books which they called a library and a kitchen fridge packed with all kinds of food. Kash doubted she'd have trouble finding something to do. If she didn't want to read, she could quite easily make herself a sandwich.

Link launched himself back down the stairs and interrupted her daydream. In one hand he held a small rucksack and in the other he held a wrist clock. The only difference was that it looked much more like a human watch.

He pressed it into Kash's palm. "You must give this to Faye when you see her. This is a timer; currently it says there is one week three days left. When the time runs out, Faye must be inside the Lamplight. A lot more is at stake than just exposing the conference to the public; make sure she wears it." Link kissed the hand he'd put the timer in. "Take care Kash, I hope to see you again someday."

Kash tried to shout, "That's great, but what do you mean you hope to see me again someday! And where's Dax?!" But Link had disappeared out of the door before he'd heard her.

Now she knew where to go and what to do, all she had to do was wait.

* * *

It's been quite a productive day, Kash thought to herself. She'd spent much of it asleep or watching movies imported from earth on their cube, but in comparison to what she'd usually do in a day, it had definitely been productive. Before she left, she'd also make sure she hid the door handle she'd managed to break off the entrance to the living room.

The time was 8:52pm exactly and Kash was ready to leave. She'd packed food and drink, some English money, a mobile phone from Earth she'd found lying around, the timer, a pair of sunglasses and a woolly hat. She heard you could never be too careful with English weather.

Kash opened the front door then remembered she hadn't asked if she needed to lock anything behind her. She reasoned that since she'd broken into the house in the first place, it probably wouldn't matter too much. On her closing it, the door panel said, "Have a pleasant trip Miss. Trix."

"Thank you," Kash replied, not quite sure if she was talking to a door or not.

The sky was in transition between the blue of daylight and the black of night. This mixture was beautiful, but Kash swiftly reminded herself that she needed to reach Earth promptly. She raced down the drive and stood in front of the closed gates. Since they weren't already open, Kash thought the most logical thing to do would be to kick them, so she did. Kash's logic didn't always follow conventional themes. As she tried in vain to physically pull the gates apart, she noticed a button to the side of them. It said in large letters, 'Please push to open'. Kash dragged her feet to the button then began muttering something like, "Why do people have gates anyway ...Stupid gates." As she walked onto the pavement, sure enough there was the streetlamp in front of her.

Normally it would be Kash watching Dax leave but now she had to do the same. She'd seen him put the patch on his neck in the past, but he'd only done this when standing in the streetlight. It couldn't be that hard to do, could it?

Prisms

Kash convinced herself it would be fine. Just think of where you wanted to go when standing in the light and you'd get there. Easy. She stepped into the pool of orange light and noticed her elongated shadow stretch along the pavement. Tearing carefully round the edge of one of the patches, she removed the adhesive sheet from the back and placed it on her neck.

For a moment nothing happened, then she thought to herself, I want to go to London. The patch on her neck tingled slightly then in a blur she was standing down a suburban street. The patch had left a circular mark with a diagonal line through it on her neck that mirrored the birth mark of someone half Maran half Human.

Once she got over the shock and sting, the first thing Kash noticed was the extreme cold. It was absolutely freezing. She'd only ever felt the same constant temperature, but now the hairs on her arm were standing on end and her teeth were chattering together. Definitely a good idea to pack the woolly hat, she congratulated herself. The sky here was pitch black with stars dotted across the empty canvas. All the colors seemed duller, but it was exciting being on a new world. Everything was so different. There was even real grass in front of some people's houses, although most of the space was taken up by tall concrete towers. Kash had seen pictures of these 'tower blocks' in school and it had amazed her that people actually lived inside them.

So this was London. She couldn't see anyone walking around so she decided it would be best to find a shop and ask someone where to go. They'd probably point her in the direction of the nearest rail.

Kash followed the road to the end, stopping to marvel at the buildings as she passed and came across a small shop called 'News of the Worlds'. The lights were on inside and through the window she could see food lining the shelves, and chocolate bars. Real chocolate bars.

Kash carefully opened the door and resisted staring at the sweets as she walked to the counter. A woman sat watching TV behind the till and Kash couldn't make out what the people on the box were saying. Empty racks where once magazines had collected on the shelves now collected dust and greeting cards.

"Yes love?" the woman said turning to Kash. She had what is understood on Earth as a cockney accent. Of course, for someone who's never come across a cockney accent before, Kash found it hard to understand her.

"Hi, could you tell me where 'Birdcage Inn' is please?"

The woman looked at her suspiciously then said, "Blimey, you've got 'n accent from the other side of the world, where you from darlin'?"

Kash tried to make sense of her. "I don't want to buy anything."

The woman laughed. "'Ere, don't you worry we get plenty of 'em experiments comin' in 'ere, I'll speak slower. What, can, I, 'elp, you, wiv, love."

This time Kash vaguely understood the last bit of the sentence, so replied just as slowly. "Where is 'Birdcage Inn'?"

It took the woman a while to reply as she tried to place where the Inn was, but she didn't recognize it. "I'm, sorry, but, I, 'aven't, got, the, foggiest."

It seemed odd to Kash that she would use a weather related term to describe her lack of information. "I am in London, aren't I?" Kash questioned.

Not sure if she was joking or not, the woman answered regardless. "Yeah, but, London's, massive, innit. You're, in, Battersea, love, and, there's, no, 'Birdcage Inn', 'ere."

"Oh," Kash said, confused as to what the difference was. On Mara, Centar and Hem were two different places. How could one place be inside the other?

"Sorry, duckie, but, you, can try, using, our, phone, to, ring, directory, if, you, want." Kash didn't know who this directory person was, but if they could help her find Faye or Dax then it would be worth a try.

"You, do, know, how, to, ring, up, 'n, enquiry, service, don't, ya?" The woman made some signals with her hand that looked like she was trying to connect what appeared to be a keypad to her ear.

When Kash didn't reply, she grabbed a phone and typed in some numbers. "Yeah, I'm looking for a 'Birdcage Inn' in London? Just the address cheers darlin'. Alright I'll wait." She smiled at Kash and drummed a set of long polished nails on the counter. "Hi, yeah okay, brilliant cheers love, bye." The woman quickly scribbled something on a memo pad and handed the paper to Kash. "It's, near, the, Barbican, love. I've, written, the, address, 'ere. Now best of British to ya. See ya later."

Prisms

It seemed like Kash's cue to go, so she left clutching the possible address of Dax and most definitely Faye. Now she knew where to go, she just didn't have the foggiest on how to get there.

Chapter 16
Lost in a Labyrinth

After finding out that not only was she wanted for terrorist activities but the removal of Caine as well, Faye had spent much of her day getting to know the resistance base. It seemed the normal thing to do, considering the normality of her day so far. The base was surprisingly large and the rooms continued deep underground. In fact, the majority of the headquarters could be accessed through the basement.

It maintained the façade of a pub and the barman would serve anyone who entered, but it was known to be the most infamous and notorious resistance base in the world. Faye thought it was just a bit daunting that she'd had no idea Dax had been a part of it. Sure, she knew he'd been messing around with some group, but nothing as heavy as this.

Mat and David seemed nice enough guys though and they'd even given Faye her own room. It was basic and small, with one bed and one desk, but they assured her she could decorate it later if she wished. The fact she could decorate it later seemed to suggest she'd be spending quite some time there and it was likely to be cramped gauging from the number of people milling around. The majority were students but there were also adults who trained prospective members.

Since it had only taken Faye until 7.00pm to get to know the base, Mat had suggested that she meet her own trainer. It was normal procedure apparently and all new members completed training in every aspect of the resistance. Faye was fine with this, but it seemed to her that it was more of a cult than a group. A cult who didn't take too kindly to strangers.

Now, she was on her way to one of the training rooms. Mat led the way down the steep barely lit basement stairs and Faye could smell the scent of musty vintage wine mixed with sawdust. She presumed it was still occasionally used as a wine cellar.

"Don't be fooled by appearances," Mat warned. "It's only a front, remember?" He walked over to one of the barrels and lifted the tap to reveal a small panel of numbers. Mat punched in a sequence of four, then the barrel lid slid slowly to one side. Inside the barrel, Faye could see little lanterns lining the walls of a rock slope that led down and away from the entrance. It was amazing because Faye thought this kind of thing only happened in books and movies.

Someone climbed down the basement steps behind them and Faye turned to see it was David holding his own glowing lantern. There wasn't anything visibly lighting it like a candle, but it gave off the impression there was.

"I thought you might need some light," David offered.

Mat reached round Faye and took the swinging lamp from his hands, giving him a knowing look as he did so. "Faye, we go quite deep underground now and I just want to let you know there's no turning back once we do. Literally because there's no room to turn round, but also, well, you know what I mean. Shall we?" Mat suggested.

Faye nodded and watched him walk up the barrel steps and disappear down the other side. She followed him and jumped lightly onto the rocky slope.

It wasn't that steep and it was an even decline from where the many pairs of traipsing feet had worn it smooth. The curved rock walls were rough, and the tunnel smelt of earth and wax. They walked down the twisting slope for about ten minutes then entered a larger area. There were several metal barrels in this cave, with three chairs lined along one wall and six doors that Faye presumed continued the twisting network of tunnels. Mat walked toward the furthest door with Faye still sandwiched in between him and David. It wasn't so much a door as it was a piece of wood with vertical slats in it. Faye couldn't see any light behind it but Mat opened it anyway. As she had predicted, it was pitch black. This new place smelt damper and felt colder than the cave they were in. Not spooky at all, then.

"Faye," Mat said turning round and handing her the lantern, "you walk on from here alone. Follow this tunnel down and you will find an open section at the end. Don't be scared, but it is a dead end."

"Oh yeah, nothing to be scared of there. You're sending me down a pitch black dead ended damp tunnel!" Fay retorted.

"You need to do this if you're going to join the resistance," Mat reminded her. "When you're at the end, stand in the middle of the space. We can't come with you past here and the experience is different for everyone who enters, but this is also how you meet your trainer. It will test your courage and your commitment to the extreme. You need to completely trust in yourself and don't doubt the choices you make. Good luck Faye."

Faye took one step forward into the dark tunnel and immediately wanted to get out. "Why would I need luck?" Faye shouted. She turned round to leave the tunnel, but found no door. It was just a cold, jagged rock wall and it seemed the only way to leave was to follow this through.

Why did you ever agree to this? she accused herself. Faye took a few more steps forward and put the lantern on the floor. She could barely see the path ahead, but it looked fairly even and didn't slope too much. Picking up the lamp, she continued into the darkness.

Faye had walked for what she guessed to be around five minutes before the lantern died. Brilliant! No light in a pitch black tunnel. Furiously she hit the lamp a few times, then gave up and dropped it on the floor. She tried to heed Mat's advice to trust in herself as she felt the walls either side of her, but had a sneaking suspicion he wasn't referring to the tunnel.

Continuing down the slope by touch alone, Faye began to feel the passage get narrower. That was weird; the walls had seemed much further apart a while back. She kept walking down the slope but the walls were definitely closing. Faye faltered for a moment then decided becoming a member of any resistance wasn't worth this.

"Hey, can someone get me out please!" she shouted to no one. The only reply she heard was her own echo; it reverberated off the walls either side of her and the volume was virtually deafening. Mental note to self, she thought, Don't EVER shout in a dark tunnel or cave again. Perhaps this was the test, she guessed hopefully. Maybe it was to withstand a sort of sensory deprivation. She couldn't see how this test would help with anything Sponsor, conference or Runner related though.

The walls were now so close, that it was a struggle for Faye to walk easily down the tunnel and the slope was gradually getting steeper. She felt her feet slip and slide underneath her and wished the lantern hadn't died. It was now so narrow that she was forced to edge along the path side-wards. Just when she thought she was stuck, Faye squeezed through a gap in the walls and found she could move her arms again. Walking tentatively forward, Faye stretched out an arm in front of her and felt another cold rock wall. She ran her hand along it and noticed that the wall now seemed to be circular and the tunnel she'd walked through had vanished.

It was just tall enough to stand up in at her height and just wide enough to touch the walls on either side all the way round. Following her earlier instruction, Faye stood completely still in the centre. She stood like this for about quarter of an hour and nothing happened. Maybe this was a cruel trick to imprison her. Faye went to sit down but felt that the floor was burning. Why then could she not feel it through her feet? Then she realized why.

Back at 'The Barrel and Barman' she'd been on her way to get the pendant and hadn't been wearing any shoes. She'd been kidnapped in the same way and Mat had given her a different pair of shoes to wear. Obviously they were somehow resistant to the heat in some way, but the lack of space and ridiculous heat made it impossible for her to sit down.

Fine. I wanted to stand anyway, she thought angrily to herself. Another five minutes passed and still nothing happened. Faye determined that she didn't even care now and that they could probably throw anything at her and she'd handle it.

Just as she began to consider this, Faye felt a shifting under her feet. Then in a second, the floor fell away beneath her and she was blinded by pure white light. Everywhere she looked was white and coming from the pitch black tunnel had made it virtually impossible to see. She picked herself up out of a heap and tried to re-orientate herself. Faye squinted through the light to find some object or surface, but instead she saw a large black tower in the distance. Stumbling a few steps forward, Faye noticed other towers around her of varying heights and they too were all polished black. She wobbled and dropped to one knee, struggling to get back up. Faye thought she heard shouting but she couldn't be sure. Before she could call for help or find the strength in her legs to make her run, there was an excruciating pain in the side of her neck and everything went black like the towers.

* * *

Faye began to come to and tried to move her limbs. She opened her eyes slightly, but it was still really difficult to see properly. Forcing them to remain open she began to adjust to the light. She was in a square room with blank white walls and the color was dazzling enough to blind someone. Faye was sat at a white metal desk when she noticed her hands were securely bound to the table, and her feet bound to the floor. Don't panic, don't panic, don't panic, she repeated to herself. Too late.

"Are you awake enough now?" a voice said snidely from behind her. It was a feminine voice that sounded like it belonged to a middle aged woman. Faye shook her head and tried to rid the pain from her neck. Everything ached and Faye had never been so terrified in all her life.

A tall, slender woman wearing all black moved gracefully round the side of Faye and sat down in the chair opposite her. It was slightly disturbing that Faye didn't have a clue where she was or who the woman staring at her was.

Faye had regained most of her vision and now looked at the menacing face of the person sitting opposite her. The woman folded her arms and placed a clipper on the table in front of her. She had golden hair and maroon eyes. Suddenly, she reached forward and attached a small cube to the rod shaped clipper.

"This," she said gesturing at the object on the table, "is a stinger. It is used as a method of torture by conference interrogators within the Lamplight." A thin hand traced along the length of the metal rod then the woman circled Faye once and stopped on her right hand side.

"You are going to answer all of my questions," the woman demanded. Her voice was hard and there was no emotion in her face.

Faye kept thinking to herself, I'm too young to be removed! She looked up into the woman's eyes, as she snapped, "Give me the names of the resistance members known to you."

This took Faye by surprise. She hesitated for a moment. "I don't belong to a resistance group, I don't know any names."

The woman glared at her. "LIAR!" She then applied the metal rod to Faye's neck. Pain spasmed through her for a few seconds and then Faye was left gasping for air.

"I don't know their names! I'm seventeen!" Faye tried to shout.

This just angered the woman. She grabbed Faye's face and shouted into it. "Don't play me for a fool girl. Tell me their location!"

Tears started to roll down Faye's face and she sobbed. "I don't know."

"LIAR!" the woman accused again. Faye again felt shockwaves of pain through her body and she writhed in agony. With her feet and hands secured, there was nothing she could do.

"Did no one ever tell you that liars are punished?" the woman questioned.

Faye tried to stay completely silent, but her breath came out in short gasps as she choked on her tears.

"I'm going to go at this from a different angle," the woman said. "We are holding your father in one of our cells and he will be removed if you do not tell me the names of your associates. You have five seconds before I give the order. Five..." the woman began to count.

"Please, please I'll ..."

"... Four."

"... I'll tell you anything ..."

"... Three."

"... else, just don't hurt ..."

"... Two."

"... him, I beg you!"

"... One."

"Okay, I'll tell you!" Faye screamed.

Tears had left tracks down her cheek and her body still burnt from the torture. The woman calmly went and sat opposite Faye, crossing her legs as she did so and placed the stinger on the table.

"Okay, Faye. If you tell me one tiny name, your father will be released. Give me the name of one person within the resistance and you can go."

Faye calmed herself down and fought back tears. Then she gritted her teeth and spat, "One name. One name you need to know. Anna Link. Even if I knew the names, there is nothing you could do to make me tell you. I stand by what I said and you'll probably remove me anyway. So bite me you old witch."

The woman stood up and walked over to Faye. Standing next to her, she held up the stinger and Faye closed her eyes waiting for the pain. When nothing happened she opened them again and found that she was no longer in the white room. It was the cave where Mat and David had left her, and she was sitting in one of the three chairs, hands placed on her lap.

Faye was physically shaking and the same woman who had tortured her now wore a pair of denim jeans and purple blouse. The hand that had been raised now held nothing and she reached down to grab Faye's own hand.

Helping her up out of the seat, the woman looked at Faye. "Welcome to the resistance, I will be you trainer for the next few days. My name … is Emma Fynn."

Chapter 17
The Disappearing Trick

"Lark stop for a sec, I can't breathe!" Clare panted.

"If we stop running they might catch us," Lark hissed back.

"Okay, here's a crazy idea," Clare said, bending over with her hands on her knees. "There is a tiny chance that we've run for twenty-five minutes straight and they might not catch us. I don't even know where we are!" she shouted.

They both stopped and looked around. It was darker now and the street lamps burnt brightly down the road lined with town houses.

"Lark, how about we find a place to stay tonight and we continue this goose chase in the morning?" Clare suggested.

"Have you been paying attention at all?" Lark snapped. "We're looking for Faye, not geese!"

Clare made a noise of exasperation and sat down on the pavement cross legged. "Fine. Then I'm not moving," she said smugly.

"No, no, no, what are you doing, get up! Look, if we find some way of getting to Piccadilly Circus then you can rest. I think I have a plan."

"Go on," Clare said, waiting to hear it. Like it would work anyway, but she'd give him the benefit of the doubt.

"Well, you know the big screens in Piccadilly Circus?" Lark asked.

"Yeah, who doesn't?"

"I don't, so you're going to show me there. Apparently, there's a conference base behind them and the Runners can use it to gather information. If we can get inside, we may have a chance of finding Faye."

Grey clouds gathered above them and small droplets of water began to fall from the sky. A twenty something man ran past covering his face with a hood.

Clare tutted. "All I ever hear is Faye this and Faye that. You know, she's not the greatest problem in the world. Next you'll be telling me the worlds are about to collide!" It was a relevant enough point to make. She'd be driven insane if they didn't talk about something else soon.

Lark glared at Clare. "Help me get to Piccadilly Circus then you can rest all you like," he barked.

"Fine," she said giving in. "Help me up and we'll find a train station."

Lark offered her his hand and they began to walk down the street. "If you'd let me lead this 'mission' in the first place, we'd be considerably further along by now."

Everywhere was completely silent. People had disappeared inside for the evening and were curled up on sofas watching TV, while Clare was running about like a lunatic in the cold London air. It was madness!

They walked for another five minutes and found themselves staring at the River Thames. Rain was falling much more heavily now and formed small ringlets on the surface of the water. Clare shrieked a few times about her hair getting soaked but was soon silenced when Lark threatened to pull his gun again.

There were few boats on the water nowadays, ever since the ferry bomb attack. One year ago, a resistance member detonated a bomb on a sightseeing boat beneath Tower Bridge. The explosion took the lives of every passenger on the boat as well as several on the bridge. After this incident, the conference banned ships over a certain height from traveling down the Thames, and the maximum number of passengers allowed on board was dropped to two people. It was a real shame that all free will seemed to be slipping away. As a young girl, Clare had loved traveling in the sea life ferry with the glass floor. Not that you could see much through the murky water but still, it was the experience of it all she enjoyed.

"Embankment is just to the right up that slope," Clare told Lark. She led the way and he followed closely behind her. As they walked past the closing bars, a homeless man sat playing something on his guitar. Normally, Clare would've walked straight past with her head down, because it was a known fact that often they were Sponsors in disguise, but Lark stopped. He clicked his fingers at Clare and motioned for her to come and listen. When she stood nearer, she noticed that the man had his eyes closed and that he was singing with the most beautiful voice. He looked like a human man in his mid-thirties, with a small goatee on his chin and short brown hair that sat under what looked like an old station master's cap. The light blue T-shirt clung to his chest and the distressed jeans covered past his worn converses.

"Listen to the lyrics, they're crazy," Lark whispered to Clare. She didn't see the point in listening to the ramblings of a homeless man and didn't approve of Lark's tone, but she stopped anyway and stood with Lark.

Whilst playing chords on his guitar, the man sung, "Is it wrong we fight like this, when words hurt less than stones and sticks. You find this girl and stop the news, but I don't see what good it'll do. You save the world, but who'll save you? The worlds collide and boom, we're through."

"He could be singing about anything," Clare huffed impatiently, and dragged Lark up the street.

It didn't take long for them to get to the abandoned tube to Piccadilly but when they got there, they found it was crawling with Sponsors. Obviously they wanted the screens well protected. Lark and Clare stayed slightly down the steps and peered through the railings toward the conference base. It didn't look much like a place of national security, Clare thought. There were what looked like two shut down shops beneath the screens and both were in darkness. This was clearly the way in, but it had been kept a well-guarded secret.

"Okay, here's what we're going to do," Lark ordered. "I'll run across first and open one of the doors. You watch which shop I enter, follow after I'm inside and I'll shoot anything else that moves, sound good?"

"I think so," Clare whispered back. "But I can't promise not to escape."

Lark ignored her and retrieved his gun. "Good, they better not get in my way," Lark hissed, then he leapt up the steps and threw himself across the road, avoiding the streetlamps. Luckily the Sponsors were all looking in different directions when he opened the shop door.

Clare waited for the guards to patrol in the opposite direction away from the shops then ran toward the two entrances. Both were next to each other and she was fairly sure Lark had opened the door on the right, so she tentatively pushed it and found it opened. Obviously that meant she was in the correct shop.

Inside, there were old catalogues and pieces of paper from before the ban. A broken office chair sat in one corner and a shattered strip light dangled from the ceiling, flickering on and off repeatedly. The peeling wallpaper looked at least ten years old and there was an old door hanging off one hinge up ahead. Clare presumed that this was where Lark had gone. She stepped through it and found herself face to face with a Sponsor.

* * *

Breaking the door down hadn't been hard for Lark. All those years of resistance training had finally come in handy. Inside, the shop was cluttered with cardboard boxes and rubbish, but there was no obvious entrance to the facility. Speed had to be on his side, it was only a matter of time before one of the Sponsors heard the noise and followed. Lark hadn't given any consideration to which shop he should enter but the one on the left had seemed more likely. Now, he just had to wait for Clare to join him and they could get going.

"Come on Clare," Lark whispered to himself. When she didn't appear he glanced at the tube station steps and saw she was gone. Damn, she went in the wrong shop! he thought. She wouldn't be so stupid to try to escape, she'd be detained in seconds.

Lark charged out the door and ran into the other shop. He was gradually beginning to panic and noticed that she wasn't inside here either. The door on the back wall swung loosely from its broken hinges so Lark kicked it open, breaking it completely. On the other side, there was a ladder stretching up to the second floor and a fire exit that Lark presumed led back out onto the street. He threw the exit door open and saw a Sponsor about twenty feet away standing in the streetlight.

There was someone with him, who Lark recognized to be Clare.

"Lark! For the love of Mara help me you idiot!"

He began to race toward the streetlamp, quickly closing the gap between himself and Clare.

As he got close enough to see the Sponsor smile, they began to disappear into the light. Lark tried to speed up but reached them too late.

He was now stood in an empty spotlight alone with his shadow, so he furiously hit the metal post. "Damn!" he shouted, running his hands through his hair and cursing.

Lark heard footsteps running toward him so pulled his gun and aimed it at the advancing Sponsor. Reaching into his pocket, he produced his badge which he then threw to the Sponsor. "I'm a Runner," he announced putting away his gun.

"Sorry to disturb you sir, have a good evening," the man apologized.

Lark wasn't quite sure why he cared so much that Clare was gone. Maybe it was purely that he didn't have leverage or someone to help him now, but maybe it was more than that. While admittedly she drove him crazy, he'd even considered the idea he might have feelings for her.

Whatever his reasons for caring, he now had two options. Follow his heart and the Sponsor into the Lamplight to rescue Clare, or follow his head and Fynn by continuing to search for Faye. Time was running out for both of them, but he would only be able to find one of them before it did. The only question, was who?

Chapter 18
Destiny's Decision

After getting over the shock of the initiation test, Faye had calmed down enough to have a coherent talk with a woman who announced herself to be her new trainer. She was being pretty presumptuous, Faye thought. What if she didn't want her as a trainer, could she even say no?

They left the three-chaired cave and exited through one of the other six doors. This time, the passages were better lit and Faye saw inside various rooms as they passed. Some had computers in and some contained equipment such as guns and disguises. Faye believed that if the Sponsors attempted to attack this stronghold, they would fail miserably.

Emma Fynn wound her way deeper into the tunnel network and stopped outside a door marked 'Observation Room'. "We can talk in here about what just happened to you and where we go from here," she said. In reality the woman had plain blonde hair, hazel eyes and was very obviously human. Faye was itching to ask her all kinds of questions, but first she wanted to find out what she'd let herself in for.

The now friendly trainer opened the door and gestured for Faye to go in. This room was a simple cave, with a large fridge in one corner and several chairs dotted around what appeared to be a dark screen that covered most of one wall. Faye sat down as far from the black panel as possible, just in case something else happened. She was quickly joined by Emma.

The woman crossed her legs and began to stare at Faye. It

wasn't a disturbing sort of stare, Faye thought. More inquisitive, as if Emma couldn't really believe she was real.

Then the woman began to speak. "Faye, what you just witnessed was the worst case scenario. The test you just undertook was designed to mirror reality inside the Lamplight precisely. From the surreal surroundings, to your brutal treatment, it was all meant to reflect what could happen to you if you're caught. For a first attempt Faye, I must say, I was extremely impressed."

Unsure if the woman was complimenting her for withstanding torture or not failing completely, Faye replied a quiet, "Thanks, I think."

"I truly mean it. Here at the resistance, however, we aim to train you so that there will be no need for you to face a situation like that again. You will attend practice sessions and simulations designed to build up your defense against Sponsors. Fairly soon, we will have the technology for you to practice against the Runners."

This worried Faye. How could she possibly hope to defend herself from someone who was virtually indestructible?

Emma continued, "Fairly soon, we will have the technology that allows us to replicate Runner like abilities. When we crack the metaphorical egg, we want to test these abilities on you."

Test them. On her. Like a terminator guinea pig? For someone who thought her world was already completely broken, Faye was again proven wrong.

She stood up and began to back away from the woman. "No, you've obviously misunderstood. I don't want to be a Runner. Why does it have to be me? Why can't you choose a better experienced resistance person? And don't give me any rubbish about it being my fate; fate comes from lies and children's playground rhymes."

Emma also stood up and raised her hands in defense. "Faye I'm not going to lie to you. I'm not going to patronize you either, but for whatever reasons, you are the only one who can use these abilities. You will be trained by the best because I am the best. There will be no room left for chance and now that you are part of the resistance, we can't afford for you to leave."

"Never? As in, you think I'll stay here forever?" Faye questioned.

"Well," Emma considered. "I mean leave the resistance as a group. You're part of the family now."

Faye was not. How dare this woman make such a ridiculous statement. How dare she throw round words like family as if they meant nothing.

Tears began to well in Faye's eyes. "My family consists of four people. Me, Mum, Dad and Dax. No one else. Two of them may be missing at the moment, but I don't want to be part of your sadistic group. You are NOT my family. You can keep this insane job offer, because I won't do it," she spat. Faye stormed away from her and turned to leave through the door. When she reached the place where it had been, there was now a rock wall instead.

"ARGH, what is with the stupid doors around here?!" Faye shouted. "You let me out of here right now or I'll ... I'll ..."

"You'll what?" Emma asked. "Sit back down again?"

Faye hated fighting an argument she knew she couldn't win. This woman clearly wasn't going to back down and she definitely wasn't going to reveal the location of the door any time soon.

"You are SO frustrating, why can't I leave!" Faye continued to shout.

Emma sat down calmly. "Because we haven't finished talking. Now please, if you wouldn't mind?" she asked, motioning that Faye rejoin her on the chairs.

Faye stood still for a second; maybe calculating her likelihood of finding the exit, then stomped back to her seat and crossed her arms. She bit her lip and tried to hold back the tears, proving that she was stronger than this woman. She hated feeling trapped and this 'trainer' was definitely pushing some limits. Perhaps she could use a chair as a weapon ...?

"Thank you. Let me tell you why you need to become a Runner, in a manner of speaking," Emma addressed the sulky young woman.

Faye looked in the other direction refusing to make eye contact, but the woman knew she was listening.

"Quite soon a decision will be made; a devastating and catastrophic decision that has been prophesied for many years and will test both worlds. Only you can influence this decision and a lot is at stake if you don't. A member of our resistance will shortly be returning here with a timer. The timer will state how much time is remaining until the decision is made and you will find out exactly what you have to do. You must follow whatever instructions you are given at that point." Emma paused and took a deep breath before she said, "Ask me any questions you have."

None of it made sense. That entire spiel the woman had just given her was absolute nonsense. Faye wasn't some all-powerful decision maker who could influence people. She had a hard time persuading her mum to lend her money, let alone anything else. There were so many questions that Faye wanted to ask and so little time apparently. She still wasn't happy with the idea.

"I can't do this," Faye said instead. "You've got the wrong person." She repeated in her head, please admit you're wrong. PLEASE realize it's all a mistake!

Emma considered this very seriously for a moment, then turned to Faye. "No, we haven't." Faye's heart sunk and she bit her bottom lip nervously.

"This is a task that you alone must complete. Faye, you're a shadow of what you're destined to become. Every event in your life has been leading up to this one moment and you have no other choice than to except it. How long do you want to spend living as a shadow in the Lamplight? How long do you think you can deny your inevitable future for? Because if you don't realize the importance of your role soon, our worlds will collide. Faye, you have the lives of your family in your hands. Just remember that when you deny your destiny."

Faye was absolutely speechless. It was still nonsense! She hated the idea of destiny and how final it sounded but she knew that people should never dice with it, regardless of whether they thought it was real or not. The 'worlds colliding' was obviously a figure of speech, but how could one seventeen year old girl have the lives of her family in her hands? Perhaps it would be best to humor Emma for now, then figure a way out later.

"I'm sorry," Faye apologized. "You talk a grand talk and you certainly walk the walk, but I'm seventeen. This doesn't happen to me. I get bad grades occasionally, I date the wrong guy, but I don't save the whole damn world. I don't believe in destiny or that I have some great role to play in it, but I do believe in family. Especially my family." Tears caught in Faye's eyes and began to fall lightly onto her dusty arm. This was half a mixture of emotion left from earlier and half the product of reluctantly attended drama lessons. "I can't promise to live up to your crazy plans, but I will go to any length to save my family. If trying my best to become this half breed Runner will help at all, then I owe that much to them; even if it is ridiculous."

Emma smiled and sighed with relief at Faye's acceptance. Her face looked less stressed and the tiny creases on her forehead had disappeared. "Thank you for believing me," Emma said sincerely. "Now please, you must have some questions?"

It had worked, Emma had taken it. Faye wasn't sure which one to ask first after that monologue, so she decided to ask the most obvious one. Wiping away the salty smudges from her cheeks, she questioned, "Are you related to Torre Fynn?"

The trainer was taken by surprise and began to laugh.

"What?" Faye asked, looking puzzled by this sudden outburst of uncontrollable laughter. Emma calmed down. "I just tell you that you alone will decide the fate of the worlds, and you ask me about my family?"

Faye herself laughed slightly and admitted sarcastically, "Yes, it seemed the least complicated."

Emma grinned and moved one chair closer to Faye, causing Faye to slide her chair slightly further back. "Torre Fynn was my husband. There was a big scandal about our relationship one year ago, but it would never have worked out. We would've had an obligation to hunt each other down every day of the year!"

"Yeah, I can see how that would ruin a relationship," Faye scoffed. She swiftly moved on to her next question before Emma realized that she didn't really have any desire to become this Runner half breed. "Do you know what this 'prophesied' decision will be? Please, be honest."

Emma was quickly focused again then replied, "Honestly? We're not sure. Only you will find that out when the time comes."

It was like a cult! The balance of the worlds rest on your shoulders and all that. Faye was still extremely confused about the whole thing, but decided that asking endless amounts of questions would confuse her even more.

She limited herself to one final question. "Why am I the only one who can change this decision? Why can't anyone else do it?"

All warmth between them, if there ever had been any, had gone and it was like two executives discussing their options at a meeting.

Emma stared at Faye then looked over to the wall. Faye followed her gaze and noticed that the door had reappeared. Then the trainer turned back and wrung her hands together before she replied, "We don't know, we only found out about one week ago. We found out from your father."

Chapter 19
Ghost Towns

Kash thought that being in London was very similar to being in multiple foreign countries all at once. The locals seemed to disappear as and when they pleased and the accents were crazy.

She stood on the corner of the high street she'd managed to find and glanced around at the closing shops. As far as she could tell, there were no Sponsors currently patrolling the streets. At least that was sort of a bonus and the weather could've been much worse, Kash assured herself.

Standing watching the world go by, Kash noticed that there were very few cars on the roads. Apparently cars were individual machines that carried people wherever they wanted to go, but Kash couldn't see many. The only cars on the road were black with little orange signs that sat on the roof. Many whizzed past, sending a flurry of air that whipped Kash's hair into a wild frenzy. They looked quite ominous, moving at such speed like little orange fireflies dancing in the night. It was a perfectly choreographed routine that allowed them to race toward each other but never touch.

Perhaps they would take other people where they wanted to go, if you asked nicely enough. This seemed like a good plan but Kash didn't have a clue how to stop one. She thought stepping into the road would probably be counterproductive, but staying on the pavement meant she'd never stop one of these machines. Deciding on a compromise between the two, she held her arm out into the road and made a stop sign with her hand as the next firefly approached. Then at the top of her lungs, she shouted, "Machine, I

116

command you to stop!'"

Taking her completely by surprise, the car pulled over and turned its little orange light off. Kash stood there for a few seconds trying to steady herself from this near death experience then saw a window begin to lower.

"You gettin' in or not?" the guy inside said.

This was something she hadn't prepared herself for. It hadn't crossed her mind that the machine would actually stop! It was all well and good that she now had a way of getting to 'Birdcage Inn' but first she had to figure out how to enter the car. Unbeknown to Kash, the modern cars required someone to push the door for it to open. Since she could see no obvious way of "gettin' in," it seemed quite plausible that trying to climb in through the front window would be acceptable enough.

Kash put her head, right arm and shoulder through the window before the driver shouted, "What you doin'! You got a screw loose or summit; use the door!"

Kash realized that the cockney man was angry due to his tone of voice, so quickly removed herself from the window and took a step backwards. She saw the man's silhouette shake his head, then one of the back car doors opened. This was a much easier way of entering the machine, Kash thought. Carefully stepping into what apparently was a 'Taxi', she sat down in one of the seats and watched the door close behind her.

"Right, at bleedin' last!" the cabbie said. "Where you goin' to?"

Kash didn't want to embarrass herself so she just handed him the piece of paper and said, "Hello. Man, I would like to go there please."

He looked at her for a minute in despair then read the piece of paper. His eyes quickly scanned the address as if searching for something then seemed to find what they were looking for.

"Yeah, sorry darlin' I live in the opposite direction. I can drop you off in Piccadilly Circus, then my house is just up the road," the taxi driver suggested.

Based on her last encounter with a person from London, Kash again decided it was much safer just to nod.

This was the only signal the man needed and Kash heard an engine roar into life. Suddenly the car shot forward, throwing Kash off the seat and onto the floor. "I'm okay!" she confirmed.

There was a knock on the glass partition and the man pointed to some kind of strap on her seat. This must be what stops people from flying around, Kash thought. Giving it a second attempt, she sat back down and tried to tie the belt in a knot around her stomach. The taxi driver must've given up, because he rolled his eyes then refocused on the road.

Being on another world was scary. Everything, when it did move, moved so fast. The taxis seemed dangerous and the people didn't even speak coherently.

Through the tinted windows, Kash saw streetlamps flick past and house lights blur as they raced along the quite London streets. The frost began to gather around the edge of the pane of glass Kash sat next to, making her pull the woolly hat further over her ears.

The man in the front shifted in his seat and reached to press some kind of button. Deafening music suddenly erupted around Kash followed by the atrocious singing of the taxi driver. It was like he was trying to compete against a screeching cat in some twisted version of a talent competition.

Earth was weird, Kash decided. It was far too strange for her liking, but different cultures still fascinated her. The only other place on Earth that Kash had heard of was France. Her father had told her ghost stories as a child about the capital city and the tower that loomed over it.

* * *

10 Years Ago.

"Kash, stop annoying your brother," her father said in a bored tone. "Look, if you want something to do, I'll tell you a ghost story if you promise to be quiet."

It was obvious that Kash's ears had pricked up and the nine year old girl ran over to where her father sat in a leather arm chair. Crossing her legs on the floor in front of the seat, she looked expectantly into her father's eyes and sat bolt upright, waiting. Lark began to sulk and eventually dragged his feet over to where Kash was, not wanting to feel left out of anything.

"Okay, now I'm going to tell you a true story about a place called Paris."

"Where's Paris, daddy?" Kash asked.

"Paris is the capital city of a place called France. France is in a whole other world where billions of people live."

"Ooooh," Kash said in awe.

"This story is about the Eiffel Tower; a big metal tower in the middle of Paris that stretches all the way up into the sky, where hundreds of people go to see the whole of France. They watch thousands of tiny dots from the top going about their daily lives, and the rivers look like snakes that twist all around the city. Some people say it's so tall, that if you jumped off the top you'd land on a cloud."

"Wowww," said the nine year old girl, her eyes alight with excitement.

"Now, it was a dark night about one week before Christmas on Earth. There were thick white clouds suspended above the black sky and the silver moon bathed Paris in tinted silver light. Many were hopeful it would snow and the air was electric with the energy of busy Christmas shoppers.

"In Paris, the Christmas lights hung from tinsel draped lampposts, shining brightly across the winding rivers. Someone had decorated the Eiffel tower so that large colorful baubles hung all the way to the top. Fairy lights wrapped around it like tiny strings of stars, there was a large red bow tied around the middle and fake snow rained down from the top of the tower.

"Jimmy had wanted to climb the tower all year, and his parents promised him that if he wished hard enough it would happen. He wished and wished with all his might, until it came true and his parents told him they would visit the tower at Christmas. When the day finally came and Jimmy got to the tower, there were big long queues that wound all the way round past little food stands and carol singers. But even though there was a very big queue, Jimmy couldn't see anyone coming back down the tower. Lots and lots of people went up, but no one came down. No wonder there's such a long queue, Jimmy thought.

"When they got to the front, Jimmy's parents asked the woman behind the counter why people were moving so slowly. The woman wore bright red lipstick and candy canes dangled from her ears. She said that the third floor was very busy and that people were stuck on the first floor instead. Jimmy thought this was a bit strange, but he still went up the tower with his mummy and daddy to look at the first busy floor. There were lots of people all pushing and shoving

119

each other to get the best view of Paris and to watch the white snowflakes twirling and dancing around each other.

"It was too crowded and he didn't like all the big people that towered over him, so Jimmy and his parents went up to the second floor. This time there were even more people rushing around, so they went up in a lift to the top floor. The third floor. Iron poles and ledges flew past as they went even higher, and Jimmy saw the tower top get even closer as they reached the entrance.

"When they got there, it was very different to what the lipstick lady had said; there was absolutely no one there. Where are all the people? thought Jimmy. His parents walked round the other side to look at another view just as Jimmy heard a noise behind him. He slowly turned round and saw a little girl standing there holding a little teddy bear. 'You shouldn't be here', the little girl sobbed. She was crying very quietly and Jimmy wanted to make sure she was okay. She should be enjoying the lovely view and pretty lights of the city. He walked over to her and asked, 'Why are you crying?'

"After he said this, Jimmy's parents heard him scream but when they searched for him, he was nowhere to be found. Jimmy and his parents were never seen again. Some say they live up there eating passing birds and don't want to come down, but they weren't the only people to go missing. Now, if you go to Paris and climb the Eiffel Tower, you won't come back down again. EVER."

Both Kash and Lark sat in stunned silence for a few seconds, then they both started crying. "No, no, no, don't cry!" their father said, trying to calm them down. "Your mother will ..."

"What have you done now!" mother interrupted, rushing down the stairs. "Aww, it's okay, whatever daddy said isn't true. He's just being a silly billy, don't worry, I'm here, I'll always be here."

* * *

A small tear began to collect in the corner of Kash's eye and she went back to staring out of the dark Taxi window. She brushed it away with the tip of her finger and thought about the story instead. After that tale, Kash had always been afraid of the place called France and its terrifying tower. She just hoped that she was very far away from it now.

Kash had lost track of how long she'd been traveling for, but the streets were beginning to change shape and houses were replaced with derelict shops. She could vaguely see a large luminous screen ahead, projecting adverts for the conference across the street.

The taxi driver stopped just outside the large screen and turned round. "That'll be £30.00."

This sounded like some form of payment was required, so Kash pulled out a note with 50 on it and handed it to the man. Then she half fell out of the open door just as the driver shouted, "Do you want the change?"

It was too much hassle to answer, so instead Kash raced down the street and stopped outside a shop called 'Underground.'

The lights in this new place were so much brighter and Kash warily watched shadows moving between the streetlamps. These must be Sponsors, she guessed. It would be safer to keep close to the walls and avoid the various spotlights. This whole adapting to a new world business was very hard.

Cogs in Kash's brain were turning like they'd never turned before as she tried to think of what to do next. Perhaps someone in 'Underground' could help her; it looked the most likely of places to find someone in. She approached the entrance and saw a set of moving stairs in front of her. Placing one foot cautiously on the top step, she found she ended up where she had started. Kash tried to walk down again but didn't get anywhere. The stairs were working against her and she desperately needed to get out of sight of the Sponsors. She quickened her pace until she was literally running, but it was pointless because she was running on the spot, trying to run down an up escalator that refused to change its direction for her.

Kash gave up and edged along the side of a shop wall instead. When she reached an open stretch of road, she straightened up and prepared to dash across it for better cover. Just as she began to move forward, she ran straight into the hard chest of a rather large man. What a great way to die, Kash accused herself. He blocked out the street light and obscured her safe passage to the other side. Slowly, she looked up at the face of the man who had stopped her and froze. Every muscle in her body was tense as she waited for him to say something. It was impossible, it couldn't be him. Her mind spun, considering the infinite scenarios that could explain his being here. None of them fitted.

She opened her lips and watched the warm air spill out into the cold night frost. He held her gaze and waited for her to say something. "Dad?" she asked.

Chapter 20
Practice Makes Perfect

How could her dad be in on all of this? He worked for the conference, not the resistance. Try as Faye may to get Emma to tell her more, she bluntly refused and told her not to keep asking questions but just except it. Yeah, thanks for nothing.

In the base, it seemed like no one ever slept. There was always someone rushing around or ducking into different rooms. Although Faye wasn't entirely sure if she was happy about being part of this group, if it helped her get her family back then it was worth a try. Plus, she may be able to knock a few heads together along the way and talk some sense into them.

After leaving the observation room, Emma had taken her to a place called 'practice'. It was a large square area with four tall white walls and absolutely nothing in it.

Faye looked confused. "How exactly am I going to learn in an empty room?"

Emma pursed her lips together. "It's not an empty room; we can accurately simulate virtually any realistic scenario. However, the appearance is only basic and the only detailed set we've managed to construct is the area inside the Lamplight." As Emma said this, large black towers seemed to form around them with one large complex in the distance. The only thing that gave away its authenticity was the lack of patrolling Sponsors.

"Are the towers physically real?" Faye asked.

Her trainer walked over to one of them and placed her hand carefully on the smooth black surface. Then, she drew her fist back and punched straight through it. "Technically, no" she replied. "On careful contact they will appear real, but sudden contact won't register. Think of them as realistic holograms. There is a 3D processor that allows us to get real depth into the room. See that complex over in the distance?" Emma signaled. "It really isn't that far away."

It went straight over Faye's head.

Thinking this over, Faye began to imagine all the possible rooms that could be designed. "So, what's the most complicated room that you've created?" Faye wondered.

Emma walked over to her and motioned for them to move back, then suddenly the River Thames appeared in front of them. Either side of the water were lampposts and buildings that had roads stretching away from them into the distance. It looked very realistic, but on closer inspection Faye could see that tiny details were wrong. Like the off-color brick work on the buildings or the pavement without cracks. Basic, but utterly brilliant.

"Faye," Emma said, quickly refocusing her. "I want you to go and stand over by that road." She was pointing at a street on the far right side of the river.

Faye jogged over to the spot and stood waiting for further instruction, regretting searching for Dax in the first place. When she looked back to where Emma had been, she was gone. Just as she considered what to do next, a loud voice echoed through the room.

"This is your practice simulation. Your task is to get from one side of the river to the other. There will be Sponsors patrolling along the pavements so stay clear of the streetlights. We will run this until you complete it to a sufficient standard. Ready? Go."

The lights along the river flicked on and six Sponsors appeared from different streets. They strolled slowly toward the river and began patrolling up and down the well-lit pavement.

Maybe if I just run they won't catch me? Faye thought. At least then she'd have a chance of out running them. Reluctantly, she counted to five in her head, contemplated how crazy the whole thing was, then raced across the pavement toward the river. She'd almost reached the bridge when she found herself detained by a Sponsor. Her arm twisted behind her and she knelt down on one knee.

Becoming increasingly frustrated, she looked up to see who it was and saw David grinning back at her.

"You have to admit, I make a good Sponsor," he joked. He released her arm and went back to patrolling the river.

Emma's voice said, "Start again from the beginning Faye."

It was going to be a long night, Faye thought.

This time she edged along the side of the buildings first then kept low to the ground and made it part of the way across the bridge before a cold object pressed into her neck. Someone's knee rammed into the small of her back and her face pressed into the near realistic concrete floor.

A strong arm lifted her back onto her feet and Faye turned to see Mat in a Sponsor's uniform. "Are you all in on this?" she asked in surprise.

Mat smiled. "Yeah, kind of. Just focus and you'll get what to do."

Faye went back to the beginning to start again.

This went on for at least two hours before she gathered the easiest way to get across was to sprint straight across the bridge. Faye got halfway then saw a line of Sponsors in front of her. She turned, gasping for air, trying to catch her breath and saw another line behind her. If she walked either way then she would most definitely be caught.

Instead of running, Faye sat down in the middle of the bridge and gestured for both lines to come forward. Her calm and collected attitude annoyed one of the fake Sponsors, and he began to charge at her. She waited until he was only a few inches away then kicked one leg out and watched him fall backwards.

Spending two hours watching how to professionally detain someone had given Faye plenty of tips. She rolled the man onto his front and held both his wrists with one hand. With the other, she took the pretend clipper and held it to the side of his neck. Because they were trying to mirror reality, the man now couldn't move. Then she turned and raced toward the finish point. Another man ran at her, so she dropped to the ground and slid along the bridge, kicking his ankle with her foot.

To her surprise he also fell, rendering a second person immobilized. "YES!" She hollered, fist punching the air then realizing she wasn't across yet. The last man standing in her way didn't move, but simply stood there waiting for her to come to him. She focused herself and tried to think of a way around him. By applying all her attention to the one man, she forgot about the Sponsors behind her. Just as she was about to move forward, she felt an arm lock around her neck and she was again on her knees.

David leant forward and whispered, "I think I win again. Faye, you really shouldn't make it so easy for us."

The man who had blocked her path turned and began walking back to his start point. David confiscated Faye's clipper and placed it in his pocket.

"You know," she said, "I've trained in martial arts. I wasn't very good at it and got kicked out after two lessons, literally, but my brother mastered it at black belt level. There's this thing he taught me that I've wanted to try out for a while. I don't know if it will work, but I'm pretty streetwise so I can probably pull it off." Faye smiled wryly and felt David's arm lock tighter around her neck and shoulder.

Emma's voice cut in and boomed. "Start again."

"Better luck next time," David said. As he began to release her, Faye grabbed the arm that was around her neck and threw the stunned man in front of her. He lay there trying to understand what had happened, then laughed in surprise as Faye took the clipper back and crouched above him.

"I can't believe that worked!" she said incredulously.

David was stunned into silence.

"I don't need luck," she grinned. "I'm sorry, but I want a rematch. I believe you are now out Mr. Sponsor."

David didn't try to get up but just started laughing instead. Laughter suited him better than the surly attitude he'd worn since she'd got there. Faye saw her chance to finish the exercise and dashed toward the Sponsor walking away from her. He was considerably taller than her, so she jumped on his back and applied the object to his neck. "Game over," she whispered.

Sprinting with such speed to the finish point, she reached it before any of the other Sponsors could catch up. Faye stood triumphantly on the other side of the river and shouted, "Suck on that Sponsors!"

Emma appeared from behind. "That wasn't fighting fair."

Unsure whether to apologize or not, Faye stood there and fumbled for an answer.

Before she could reply, Emma continued, "So well done. You

thought like the Sponsors would and that is the quality of a good resistance member."

"Thanks," Faye muttered back, presuming she must've forgotten that she'd actually lost in the first place.

Emma gestured for someone to join them and Faye looked round to see David sauntering toward them.

"David, Faye is ready," Emma announced triumphantly.

"Yeah I can see that. How did you learn how to throw?" he pointed out.

Faye shrugged it off, shaking her head saying, "I don't think I'm quite ready just yet."

Emma considered this then placed both her hands on Faye's shoulders. She looked into Faye's unsure eyes. "You are more than ready. You and David will go into the Lamplight and gather information on the Runners. With the information you gather, we will be able to destroy Fynn once and for all."

Chapter 21
Three's a Crowd

Kash stood in silence. This wasn't possible, this man didn't exist anymore. She was face to face with the man who had murdered her mother, and who had apparently been removed. But obviously, he was still very much alive and stood looking at his only daughter.

Torn between wanting to hit him square between the eyes and curl up into a tiny ball on the floor, Kash turned to walk in the other direction. She didn't want to talk to the one person who had made her life a misery. As she turned to leave, he caught her arm and pulled her down into the underground.

Half carrying her, half dragging her down the steps, her dad stopped at the bottom and went to say something.

Kash interrupted with, "Don't you dare apologize. I don't want anything from you, you monster. You can't just appear as part of my life again. I've moved on. I want nothing to do with you. You're a criminal!"

The man's face fell, but then hardened again. "I don't blame you." His voice was deep and the stubble on his chin suggested he was beginning to age. He wore a torn leather jacket, pair of denims and was an unrecognizable shadow of what he used to look like.

Kash wasn't sure what to say next. "Why did you let people believe you'd been removed? Why did you let your family think you were dead?"

His gaze dropped to the floor and what looked like tears began to collect in the corners of his eyes. It could just easily have been a trick of the light. "It was the easiest way. If I was gone, then I couldn't hurt you again."

Kash spat back. "Easiest? You hurt me more by running away and murdering mum." Her dad turned and slid down against the station wall. "You know what? I don't have anything I want to say to you!" Kash hissed. She turned away and began to walk back to the steps.

Her dad clasped his hands in front of him. "Your mother's ... death. It wasn't my fault. It was an accident and she got caught in the crossfire. I loved her very ... very much." He began to sob. "And I couldn't bear to lose any more of my family. I thought ... if I left, then I would cause you less pain."

Kash kicked the side of the wall and sobbed back. "I needed my dad there, to be with us, to help us through her death. But you weren't there. We coped on our own and lost another parent. How the hell do you think that made us feel, huh? Losing the two people who are meant to protect you in the world?" she accused. Tears fell lightly onto the ground and Kash paced along the side of the wall.

"I'm so sorry," her dad whispered.

Kash looked at the broken man and sat down opposite him, trying to decide what she should do next. "Why are you here dad?" she said.

He dried his tears. "You need to know that you're in danger and so is Lark."

"Everyone's in danger!" Kash shouted.

He motioned for her to keep her voice down and she slightly lowered it.

"The whole damn world is in danger! Why are we suddenly any different?" Kash snapped.

He dropped his hands between his knees and said, "Because your uncle's been removed, or had it slipped your mind."

Kash looked puzzled. "Jon?"

"Yes, have you not been watching the news? Now we have no protection and if Fynn controls either you or Lark, we would have a hell of a lot to worry about," her dad warned.

"Jon's dead?" Kash asked, a fresh bout of tears coming on.

"Yes. Fynn has replaced Jon with himself. Jon Caine's been removed and as part of his family, you and Lark are in danger. Now where the hell is Lark?"

* * *

Lark hated the idea of leaving Clare to face her fate alone in the Lamplight, but if he didn't find Faye soon, it was his life that was on the line.

He headed back toward the derelict shop and placed one foot on the first rung of the ladder. If he chose to follow this path now, he couldn't go back on his decision. This was the only two pronged road he'd be facing for a while.

Placing one foot in front of the other, Lark continued climbing until he reached the second floor. He heaved himself over the ledge and onto a metal walkway. Across it was a steel door and finger print pad that Lark walked over to and used to open the entrance.

A voice stated, "Identity confirmed. Runner Lark Lyre."

The giant door slide open to reveal a security desk with one Sponsor behind it. The woman stood up. "I'm going to need to see some form of ID, sir."

Lark reached into his pocket and produced his badge.

The woman studied it and remarked, "You're a Runner?" Lark nodded and the Sponsor continued. "Whoa, you're the first one of them I've met! Is it true you can't die or something?"

Snatching the badge back, Lark continued straight ahead. "Don't you have more important things to be worrying about?" he hissed.

The next door slid open to reveal a huge bank of TV screens. He presumed they were all forms of surveillance hidden behind the large luminous screens out front. About twenty Sponsors sat behind the screen banks, each carefully scanning one of the TVs or quickly tapping away on computer keyboards.

Lark went over to the nearest Sponsor and flashed his badge to them. "I need all known recent locations of Anna Link, including possible future destinations and places of positive ID." The Sponsor begrudgingly agreed and Lark watched as thousands of faces flashed across the screen until the computer found a match.

An address in Covent Garden appeared then the screen went blank. "I'm sorry sir," the Sponsor apologized, "no recent locations were found. It's like she's disappeared or dropped off the radar."

"Damn!" Lark shouted, much to the surprise of the working Sponsors. "Okay, do the same search for Clare Fynn."

Prisms

Again the Sponsor agreed, if not more hesitantly this time, then said, "She's currently being processed inside the Lamplight. She's in a holding cell waiting for questioning."

"Oh for the love of Mara!" Lark shouted even louder this time. "Can't anyone just stay put for one second?"

The Sponsor looked at the computer embarrassed. "Is there anything else I can do for you sir?"

Lark hit the desk and stormed out the first door. Just as he was about to leave, a siren went off and the individual screens formed into one large image. On the board, Kash was trying unsuccessfully to hide behind the underground station wall.

"Threat identified as Kash Trix, also known as Kash Caine," one Sponsor informed the room. Lark couldn't quite believe what he was seeing. There on the multi-sized screen, was his Maran sister Kash. How did she get to Earth? He knew if Sponsors were sent out after her, then she'd most definitely be removed for illegal activities.

"I will neutralize the threat," Lark shouted.

One of the Sponsors went to press an alarm button and Lark quickly removed his gun from his holster, flicking off the safety catch, holding it to the Sponsor's head. "I said I will neutralize the threat," Lark spat.

The quaking Sponsor picked up a phone and spoke down it. "Continue patrol, we are sending someone down to deal with the threat."

Lark ran toward the steel door and pressed his finger hard into the ID panel. The door slowly opened, much to his annoyance. "Come on, come on, hurry up!"

When the exit was clear, Lark slid down the full length of the ladder and bashed through the fire exit door. Full out sprinting across the street, he reached the front of the shop and looked over to the underground wall.

Kash was gone.

* * *

"How can we be in danger, we're no threat to anyone!" Kash questioned.

Her dad stopped her mid thought. "Listen, I don't know if they will bother sending anyone after you, but they will either try and

131

question you or control you. Either way, you need to get as far from here as possible."

Still in shock and entirely confused, she produced the timer and address from her pocket to show it to him. His eyes turned dark and he pointed to the counting down watch.

"Where did you get that?" he snapped.

Kash didn't know whether she was allowed to tell him so she just shrugged. Her dad stood up and dragged Kash up by the collar of her top.

"Where did you get this?" he shouted into her face.

Kash tried to say something but then remembered what Link had said to her. Besides, her father's eyes were dangerous and this now violent man scared her. She shouldn't have expected anything different from a murderer, even if it was 'accidental'. As she struggled, pressed against the wall by her father's own hands, she could hear footsteps running above them.

Her dad released her and quickly took the address out of Kash's hands. "Right, you take this line," he said pointing to a tube map behind her, "and change here to get to that address. Don't trust anyone; keep this timer well out of sight."

While Kash tried to make sense of her father's sudden outburst, she noticed him disappearing into the dark of the station and out of sight. What was it with people disappearing around here! Kash turned suddenly and saw a pair of feet running down the steps toward her.

* * *

She couldn't have got far, Lark thought. The only place she could possibly have gone was inside the underground. Keeping his head down, Lark darted across the empty road to the underground and heard voices inside. Then he heard footsteps running further into the station, followed by complete silence. No one could outrun him.

Taking the stairs two at a time, Lark virtually flew down them and stopped only centimeters away from his sister.

Kash looked surprised and shocked to see him. Lark was completely aware of the fact she was here. In her hand she held a small piece of paper and a human watch.

"Lark?!" she questioned. Her jaw fell open. She scanned his face taking in all the changes and decided it was definitely him. "Oh my God, I've found someone I know!" she shouted as she threw her arms around her bewildered brother. "How come people keep leaving then reappearing again! How did you get here?" Kash asked suspiciously.

Noticing that she was wearing a neck patch, he replied, "Oh, I got a patch from your fiancé a while ago and just took it off when I got here. I see you did the same thing," Lark noted.

Still cautious of him she said, "Yeah, but I didn't know you knew about Dax's trade? You look so different by the way, what's going on with that little beard thing?"

"I like it," Lark shrugged. "So anyway, where are you going?"

Kash decided it was probably safe enough to trust her own brother and showed him the paper she was holding. "I'm trying to find this girl Faye, she's Dax's sister, you might know her?"

"What a coincidence!" Lark beamed. "I'm trying to find Faye as well."

Lark noticed alarm bells ring in Kash's head but pretended not to see.

Now even more suspicious, Kash said, "How odd. Well, that's her address and I need to find her quickly." Kash subtlety pocketed the watch and smiled sweetly at her brother.

"Well, do you know how to get there?" Lark asked hopefully. Kash just nodded and let Lark take her arm as he led her into the dark station.

Everything was falling into place. Now all Lark had to do was bide his time and he'd be shown right to Faye's front door. That would give him enough time to get Clare back. If anyone got in his way, he'd kill them.

Chapter 22
Paralyzed

Torre Fynn was now officially the most powerful man in the whole world, not only on Mara but Earth as well. While he enjoyed having the freedom to control people at will, he also reveled in the opportunity to make significant decisions on his own authority.

Currently, Fynn sat behind a large marble desk stroking his grey beard. His dark eyes were deep in thought and the lead Sponsor sat in front of him, carefully sipped from a glass of whisky. It was far too strong but the Sponsor feared what would happen if he stopped drinking. It had got to a stage where Torre Fynn could have people killed with so much as a look.

Taking the Sponsor by surprise, Fynn batted the drink out of his hand and clicked his fingers. Someone came rushing in and swept away the broken glass, immediately replacing the whisky.

"That's what I like about this job," Torre said deliberately. "I can do anything. I can break people, destroy them, crush them and the mess will all get swept up by someone else."

The Sponsor gulped and sat in complete silence, watching the power hungry leader with careful eyes. He had no idea why he'd been called to Fynn's office, but if the Sponsors had slipped up then he'd have to take the rap for it. In fact, he'd only been lead Sponsor for about one week. The last one had been removed for having an un-ironed blazer.

"Now that Clare is again in my custody and Lark has almost neutralized the threat, I feel I am ready to start the ball rolling with our replacement plan. I'm sure you understand the importance of this?" Fynn questioned.

Without hesitation the man quickly answered, "Of course sir."

"Good," Fynn confirmed. "Then I'm sure you will support me in my latest idea. In order to perform a smooth change over from Sponsor to Runner, I think it is necessary to temporarily suspend the actions of the public." He relaxed back in his chair and crossed his arms.

The Sponsor shifted nervously in his seat. "I will support you however I can sir. Tell me my orders and I will carry them out with the utmost precision."

"Oh I don't doubt your precision," Fynn said. "It's whether you will find them morally correct that I doubt."

Looking down at the table, the Sponsor said nothing and waited to hear Fynn's plan.

"Half of the Sponsors in both worlds will be converted to Runners, half of them will be removed. This process will be your complete responsibility; I take no part in it whatsoever. For the next five days we need to temporarily paralyze every member of the population, other than conference affiliated members, to efficiently perform the changeover. On Monday, all the Runners will be active and the switch will be expertly managed. Do you agree?"

Knowing he had no other option, the Sponsor nodded and said through gritted teeth, "Of course sir. I will remove half of my men."

"Wonderful," Fynn beamed. Then he waved for the lead Sponsor to leave and started scribbling on a note pad with a gold plated pen. The Sponsor bowed and hurriedly left the office.

An hour passed and Fynn called his board of executives to a meeting.

He stood and addressed them. "Fellow conference members. In a moment I will release a nerve gas into the atmosphere that will paralyze every member of the public other than Sponsors or Runners. The members of conference inside this building and inside bases across the world will be immune, thanks to the toxins injected into your systems during our routine health checks. When I release it, every person will be paralyzed commencing from midnight tonight until midnight Sunday, five days total. The nerve gas is flawless. Our recent advances in science have made this incredible feat possible and I have no doubts about its success.

"I wish you all the best of luck with the changeover and I do not want to be disturbed until the switch has been made. Now get to work."

With that, he pressed a large red button on the table in front of him and the odorless, colorless nerve gas was released into the atmosphere of Earth and Mara. The big red button was just a perk of the job.

Everyone stopped what they were doing and froze in that position. People jogging, fell. Cars stopped mid three-point turn and crashed. Resistance planning was put on hold as every person in the world was paralyzed while the conference performed its morally corrupt change.

Fynn smiled and took another sip of whisky.

* * *

"I really don't think I'm prepared," Faye said.

Emma looked at her reassuringly. "You'll do fine. You've got all the equipment you need and David will be with you every step of the way."

David squeezed Faye's hand and went to open the door. His hand froze on the handle while Faye stopped in her tracks. She still gripped David's palm and Emma was mid-way through picking up a supplies bag with the help of Mat.

Everyone stayed frozen in their timeless five day existence.

* * *

"Lark I can't jump a barrier, it's wrong!" Kash shouted. "Anyway, it's too much effort."

Lark huffed and walked back to his sister. Just as he reached her, she froze with her hands either side of the ticket gate. Her eyes were wide open and one foot was raised as if to jump halfheartedly, but she was completely still.

Lark waved his hand in front of her face but she didn't respond. He launched himself back over the barrier and ran up the steps to check if it had happened to anyone else. All the Sponsors were still patrolling the streets and none of them appeared frozen. Then he noticed that on the large luminous screen a message read "Temporary paralyzation of all non-conference members. Duration; five days."

It was obviously some ploy by Fynn but without Kash's knowledge of exactly how to reach Faye and without the leverage of Clare, Lark was stuck for a long five days.

* * *

"You are dismissed," Fynn ordered. He sat back in his chair and grinned as people rushed around him fulfilling his orders. He was safe in his little bubble of calm while chaos ensued around.

"Oh I do love being ruler of the world," he said, smiling to himself and settling in for the five day long switch.

Chapter 23
Five Days Later

"Don't forget the supplies!" Emma shouted, just catching Faye and David as they walked through the door. The bag contained torches and guns among other such things and while Faye couldn't actually fire a gun, David was a seasoned pro.

He climbed the sloping path to the entrance of the barrel with Faye in tow. The mission was simple enough. Get in, get Runner information, get out. All in all it should take them twenty minutes tops.

Both Faye and David were dressed in fake Sponsor uniforms that had come from one of the costume rooms. Faye had ignored the sequined catsuits she'd caught sight of in the back; it was best not to ask in those kind of situations. They carried authentic badges that had only been manipulated slightly and looked completely professional. As long as the guards didn't stare at Faye for too long, they were bound to succeed.

The barrel door slid open to reveal the dark musty wine cellar once again. Everything was moving so quickly and she had so easily got caught up in this whirlwind of secrets and lies. It was hard not to go along with it and get carried away. The only risk was that she might lose herself in the process and she was fast running out of ideas to escape.

David glanced at her face and saw the tension in her locked mouth. He stopped walking halfway up the basement steps so that light fell across him and cast long shadows into the cellar. Faye couldn't see his face, but she thought that at this moment it was kind of comforting that she couldn't. If she saw fear in his eyes then she would most definitely freak out, break down, or a combination of the both.

David leant forward and whispered in Faye's ear. "You'll be fine, I promise to protect you. I've done this thousands of times so it's routine to me."

Faye still wasn't convinced and David could see in her eyes that she was holding back. "Do you trust me?" he asked softly.

"Yes," Faye replied and felt one of his hands brush along her collar bone and rest on her cheek. It was warm compared to the chill of the dank cellar and reassuring enough to convince Faye that she wouldn't be alone.

"Close your eyes," he whispered. Faye barely heard his voice as she closed her eyes. His other hand slipped from hers and held the back of her head.

She felt him run his hand through her hair and found his face was only inches from hers. She couldn't see, but felt his breath on her lips just before they kissed. For a few brief moments, Faye knew she was safe. The troubles outside didn't exist and it was only him and her in the world; two pieces of a puzzle that fitted perfectly together.

When David gently pulled away Faye kept her eyes closed, lingering on their embrace.

"If you stood on top of the tallest Lamplight tower and fell, I wouldn't be the one to catch you," David said. "I'd be the one who jumped with you. Just remember that when we're inside."

Faye smiled and could just about make out his face in the silhouette. Sure, it would be a lie to say she hadn't considered David, but it seemed kind of out of the blue. Was it really the place, or time?

"I will be with you every step of the way," David confirmed as he squeezed her hand again. An unusual display of emotion for someone so... military.

David stepped into the light of the bar and Faye saw a different man. Not just some guy in the resistance, or a random friend of Dax, but someone who was genuine. He cared for her.

"If we go now we'll make it back for an early breakfast." David grinned.

They virtually ran through the pub door into the cold night air.

Tiny stars were dotted across the sky and clouds gathered around the moon like a silver scarf. One street light stood in front of them just waiting to be used, so David pulled Faye forward until they were engulfed in the orange pool of light.

Then Faye remembered. "How exactly are we going to get there? I mean, you can't use a patch or anything and Dax isn't around to help you get there?"

David reached into his blazer pocket, producing a small prism that hung from a silver chain and refracted all the colors of the spectrum.

"My pendant!" Faye gasped. "To be honest I completely forgot about it."

David dropped it carefully into Faye's palm. "Only you can use it. Just twist it and you'll find yourself in the Lamplight. Don't let go of my hand though, or you'll be on your own."

Faye held the curious looking pendant in front of her and watched as it spun back and forth, twisting and turning in the light. "This is where it begins David. Seriously, I don't think I'm ready." Faye worried.

David took her face between his hands. "You are. This is the beginning, but how can you end something if you don't start it?" This was either a fantastic philosophical remark or unsolvable riddle, but whatever it was it did the trick.

Holding her breath, Faye grasped the prism in one hand and twisted it with the other. The ground began to shift underneath them and the London Street dissolved into brilliant white light. The pub transformed into a shiny black tower, while the pavement became as white as snow. Surprisingly, it was very similar to the set Emma had showed her earlier.

"Okay, now try to look important," David joked. He let go of her hand and his face turned completely serious. It was hard and emotionless as he led the way to the main complex. Faye began to follow but noticed something wasn't right. There were absolutely no Sponsors patrolling the Lamplight, so where were all the guards in such a high security complex?

As they approached the main tower, two men stood in front of it. They wore a T-shirt with a stripe down each sleeve that didn't match the uniform of a Sponsor. Somehow they'd missed something, or the guards had got a new uniform recently that the resistance hadn't been informed about.

"David something's up," Faye hissed.

He looked round at her and said out of the corner of his mouth, "What?"

Faye tilted her head toward the two men on guard. "I don't think they're Sponsors or regular guards."

David faced back to the tower and kept walking with his face focused. "It's probably nothing," he reassured her.

It's just routine, Faye repeated to herself as they neared the militant looking men. Their eyes were wary of the newcomers and they both exchanged a cautious glance. David motioned for Faye to stop and he walked over to the tower entrance.

"We request access to the information archives," David said in a confident voice. He handed over his fake badge and kept face while they checked it.

"You know, that is funny," one of the men said menacingly.

David looked confused. "I'm sorry I don't quite follow, what's funny?"

The guard reached for something in his back pocket at the same time David got ready to pull his gun.

"Well, Mr. Fynn ordered a five day replacement program to permanently remove all Sponsor positions. Those left were converted to Runners, so the only explanation is that you two aren't really Sponsors at all." The man's opal eyes looked over David. "Nice try."

It didn't make sense, Faye thought. Panic rose in her chest.

"Faye, run!" David shouted as he tried to pull his gun. The Runner was much quicker and applied some sort of clipper to David's neck before he could. Faye saw him crumple to a heap on the ground as the other man began to run at her. He had lightning reactions and had closed the gap between himself and Faye in seconds. Tears began to streak down her face as she took one last look at the man she'd failed to protect. Now it was all her fault.

She quickly twisted the pendant just as the Runner reached for her. The towers evaporated back into the London Street and she fell to the floor in despair. In hysterics, she just sat in the orange spotlight accusing herself. She could vaguely make out voices around her then saw Emma came into vision.

"Faye, were you followed?" she shouted urgently. "Faye!" When she received no comprehensible reply, Emma ordered, "Smash the streetlight. I don't care how, just smash it quickly or they'll find us!"

Faye listened as glass broke above her and watched as tiny shards of glass rained down around.

"Where's David?" Emma asked very calmly. "Someone get her up and inside, we can't have her wandering about the streets!" she barked again.

Faye felt a pair of arms lift her away from the dead streetlight and back toward the inn of hurt and pain. Through the tears she saw a new face come into view.

As Faye tried to speak, the face said, "Don't say anything, just rest."

Faye studied the calm pair of eyes and managed to whisper, "I know you."

The girl who was carrying her smiled and wiped away the tears with the back of her sleeve. "Shhh, just don't worry. It will all be over soon," said Kash in a comforting voice.

The ironic thing was that she couldn't have been more wrong if she'd tried.

Chapter 24
The Terrible Truth About Lyres

Kash lifted herself a couple of inches off the ground. "No, I'm sorry. I can't jump it." She looked round for Lark and noticed that he was now standing next to her. Hadn't he been standing in front of her? "Why are you standing there?" she asked, confused by his sudden burst of speed.

Lark considered this for a moment. "I haven't moved anywhere. I was about to help you over the barrier, but if you don't want my help then I'll jump it instead!"

For a few seconds Kash looked suspiciously at her brother then gave in. "Fine, help me then."

They took the line that Kash said would take them to the address and found the journey only took fifteen minutes. The twisting tube network seemed to take an age to get to the Barbican and both of them became irritated with the slow moving train. Fluorescent lights flickered on and off to the rhythm of the train.

When they stepped onto the platform, all the walls were painted white. There were no peeling posters or old advertisements plastered along them, just the occasional black symbol here and there. Kash stole a quick glance at the side of Lark's neck and noticed there was a mark on it; similar to Dax's birthmark but with another diagonal line through it. The mark matched the symbols on the station walls. His opal eyes were burning and for once in her life, Kash didn't feel safe being around her younger brother.

Helping her over the barrier again, Lark walked to the entrance of the underground and stopped. The air was calm and the world felt at peace. No one patrolled the pavements, but he knew where the real change had taken place. The Runners had shut down virtually every shop and forcibly closed those that refused. Broken glass littered the street from the lamps they'd smashed in victory and the windows they'd broken in spite. An all-powerful race of people had come, and they were demonstrating their complete control everywhere.

Kash took what looked like a mobile phone out of the bag she was carrying and held it out in front of her.

"What's that for?" Lark asked, studying the human device she was holding. She tutted at him and answered, "It's got an old fashioned SatNav built in. Apparently if you type in the address, it will show you where to go." She keyed a post-code in and began to walk along the street. As she did, she noticed the derelict shops and smashed lamps around her. "It looks like there's been a riot here," she said off hand.

Lark said nothing and clenched his jaw together. She was bound to find out the truth soon, but for now it was irrelevant.

They walked for another ten minutes until they found 'Birdcage Inn'. It was located down a dark alleyway and sat among several disused looking houses. A solitary streetlight stood outside the Inn and lit the rusting sign that hung from the wall. It looked old and tired.

"That's the place," Kash confirmed.

Lark strode ahead in front and stopped with one hand on the door. "Whatever happens from now, I want you to know that I care about you a lot. Just, don't forget that," Lark said quickly. Then he threw open the entrance and stepped inside to find a virtually empty bar. It was definitely the right place but maybe they were all out or something.

One woman sat at a table in the corner chewing her nails and glancing anxiously at her watch, while the innkeeper stood drying glasses and wiping the wood down. It didn't look anything like the most infamous resistance base in history.

Kash knew she had to deliver the timer here, but she didn't want to do it in front of Lark. For the most part she trusted him, but there was something about him that was a little off.

Lark marched over to the man behind the bar and leant forward and whispered in his ear. "We are here about Faye. We need to talk with her."

The man disappeared behind the bar for a second, then reappeared holding a shotgun. "Who are you?" he demanded, cocking the weapon he was holding.

This sudden action caught the attention of the woman in the corner and she walked over to stand directly behind Lark. He felt her literally breathing down his neck as she pulled a small pistol and held it to the back of his head. "What are you doing here?"

Kash turned slowly to face her with her hands up. "My name is Kash Trix and I have an important message for Faye."

The woman studied her face carefully then spun Lark round to face her as well. "You're Caine's children," she said in a surprised voice.

Kash bit her lip and replied, "Well, technically yes, but we're Spire Caine's children, not Jonathon Caine's. Now please don't kill us!"

The woman lowered her gun. "I think we have a common aim. My name is Emma Fynn, ex-wife of Torre. He is the one who removed your uncle."

Kash stood there shocked by this revelation. She went to say something, but the woman cut in.

"We want to destroy Fynn completely and this girl Faye is helping us."

Kash decided the woman was probably insane but that she should humor her for now.

Kash informed her. "I actually know Faye a little. You see, I'm Dax Link's fiancé, you might know him?"

The woman clicked for the barman to similarly lower his gun and proudly announced, "Dax is a key member of our resistance, so you will have our protection here." She led both Kash and her brother to a corner table and looked cautiously into Lark's eyes.

"We are awaiting her arrival; she is currently inside the Lamplight gathering information on the Runners. The only problem is, that the Lamplight runs on a time different to our own. One hour on Earth may only equate to one minute in the Lamplight. It's very temperamental," Emma said.

Lark shifted nervously and tried his best not to look guilty.

Noticing him fidgeting, Kash asked, "Emma could I talk to you in private for a sec? Lark, I hope you don't mind."

He shook his head and relaxed back into the wooden chair.

Emma gestured that she should join her walking toward the bar, then revealed a trap door and stairs that led down into the wine cellar. It was very dark and damp inside the basement and Kash could only make out the woman's shadow. Not at all ominous. When they were down the steps, the trap door slammed behind them and Emma produced a small orange lantern. It cast just enough light to make out the detail in their faces.

Kash reached into one of her pockets and pulled out the timer. The little red digits flashed '5 DAYS' and she hit it a few times to make sure it was working. That was odd. It had said one week three days remaining not too long ago.

Emma suddenly grabbed Kash's wrist. "How did you get this?"

Thinking it would be safer just to tell the angry woman, Kash replied, "Frazer Link gave it to me. He said I had to deliver it to Faye and that it's vital she's inside the Lamplight before the timer runs out. That's all he said. Is he a member of the resistance too?" Kash asked warily.

Emma took the counting watch off her and began to walk back up the stairs. "Does your brother know you have this?" she said urgently, shaking the timer slightly in her hand.

"No, but what's it for? You haven't even answered my last question!"

Abruptly Emma stopped and held the lantern up to her face. "Yes, Faye's father is a rogue member of the conference turned resistance and this timer indicates how long is left until the decision is made. It is absolutely essential if Faye is to succeed." Emma threw the trap door open and hid the timer in her pocket as she did so.

Someone who looked like a student rushed over to the woman as she stepped into the bar gasping. "Faye ... outside ... streetlamp!" she said in between short, raspy breaths.

"Kash come with me, Lark stay here and don't touch anything," Emma ordered. They raced outside and saw Faye sitting on the pavement in absolute hysterics. She was muttering something in between crying fits about someone called David, but it was hard to make out what exactly.

Kash heard Emma shout for someone to smash the streetlamp then demanded that someone take Faye inside. Kash ran over to the sobbing girl and put Faye's arm around her own shoulder. Trying to calm the girl down, she kept talking to her but didn't reply when Faye claimed that she knew her.

They walked back into the pub and Emma closely followed. "Sit her down on that chair," she directed to Kash. Kash followed her gaze and helped the girl into a hard backed velvet chair. Offering her a tissue, she continued to dry the tears that were matting in Faye's hair.

Emma dashed over to them and pulled up a chair next to where Faye was sitting. The hysterical girl was slowly beginning to calm down and managed to sob, "David, I've lost him. It's all my fault."

It was a truly pitiful sight to see, but Emma needed information about what had happened. She took Faye's face between her hands and held it until she was sufficiently calm enough to talk to. Then Emma spoke softly. "Faye, just tell me exactly what happened."

Faye sniffed a few times then said, "We went into the Lamplight and everything was fine, then there were no Sponsors. The men said they were Runners and they put something in David's neck and he fell and ... and ..." Faye struggled as tears began to well again. "... and now it's my fault that he's gone. They've got him, they know about us."

If this was true then the resistance was definitely in trouble. Emma's face was completely serious. "What did you do after that?"

Fighting back her emotions, Faye wailed, "I twisted the pendant and came back without him. It's all my fault!"

As she finished her sentence, Lark began to walk over to see what all the commotion was about.

"What did these Runners look like, Faye?" Emma asked in a concerned voice.

Faye opened her eyes and looked into the face of her trainer. Over Emma's shoulder, a man stood looking at her with curious eyes. Faye glared at him and pointed and accusing finger in his direction, then spat, "They looked like him."

147

Chapter 25
Trapped

Everything was beginning to unravel right in front of Lark's eyes. How could this girl possibly recognize him! She was the key. He needed to get her alone.

"I can explain," Lark offered warily, as he felt a pair of arms twist his behind his back.

The woman Emma turned to him. "You get one shot at explaining. I suggest you make it count."

Lark took a deep breath in as Kash shook her head. "It's not true. Lark, tell me it's not true," she pleaded.

Emma took out her pistol and again pointed it at his head.

He looked around at the furious, confused faces. "I am a Runner."

Kash began to cry and one student even pulled out a gun.

"But," he continued, "I am a member of the Hem resistance group on Mara. I infiltrated the conference to gain information and then became a rogue Runner. I thought if I told you, then this would happen." He gestured to his detained arms and bit his tongue as he waited for their reply.

Emma stared at him for a while then demanded, "If you truly are a rogue Runner, you will go to Hem and bring several resistance members back with you to clarify this. You have one hour from now, so I'd recommend that you run. That shouldn't be a problem for you, Runner," she hissed.

Lark nodded and felt his arms release.

Kash was still trying to make sense of the situation as he looked at his sister once more and headed for the door. It wasn't the fact they might kill him he was worried about. After all, he was nigh on invincible. It was the fact that if he tried to take Faye with him, they'd definitely shoot him. That'd be a horrible inconvenience. He felt a new plan beginning to formulate in his head as he raced through the exit and out of sight.

Emma turned back to Faye and was just about to say something when there was a loud beeping sound, like a digital alarm clock or an oven timer.

"Everyone check their pockets," Emma ordered. In turn, all the students emptied out their possessions until Emma was the last one left. She checked hers and pulled out the timer Kash had given her. The red digits no longer flashed five days remaining. Instead, the beeping signaled that there were three hours left.

"That's impossible!" Emma hissed. "How can the time change so suddenly?!" She caught sight of Faye staring at the watch. "You must be inside the Lamplight before this timer runs out. You MUST destroy Torre Fynn. What have you done differently? Why has the time changed? What's changed?"

Taking the watch from Emma, Faye turned it over in her hands. "This is my dad's watch. He bought it a while ago on Earth when he met my mother. How did you get this?"

Kash thought it seemed like a good moment to interject. "Your dad gave it to me; I was looking for Dax when I ran into him. He said it was very important I gave it to you and that … he loves you very much."

Frazer Link being sentimental was very odd, so something serious must be happening for him to be showing any emotion. As Faye continued to watch the timer count down, something registered about what Emma had said.

"Hang on; I thought I had to stop the decision or something. Since when has my mission been to destroy Fynn?" Faye asked cautiously.

Emma's face turned cold and her gaze hardened. "Torre Fynn made my life a misery. He is a coward to banish me from his life and a tyrant that must be stopped at all costs. He forbade me from ever seeing my daughter. You have NO idea how much pain he caused me. You are the only one who can access the Lamplight with the pendant and you must destroy Fynn. Now, if you would just stop

149

the world from revolving around you for a second, perhaps you could see that."

This was all wrong. Emma was corrupted by her want for revenge and Faye was beginning to question just what the aims of the resistance were. Her task was to stop the decision, not kill the world's leader and while Faye knew Emma was being ridiculous, she wouldn't have dared tell her.

Instead, she settled on a compromise. "Emma, you're either obsessed with destroying Fynn or getting even, either way it's all about him. Those aren't the ideals of the resistance I know, so I'm sorry, I can't be a part of your stupid plot for revenge." As Faye went to stand up, she found a pair of hands on her shoulders pushing her back into the seat. Emma directed her gun toward her. What was it with her and guns!

"How dare you do this!" Faye shouted. "You have no right to keep me here!"

Emma leant toward her, placing both hands either side of Faye's chair. "Oh, you're not going anywhere sweetheart. Not until you are given the Runner abilities necessary for you to properly enter the Lamplight. Fynn will be destroyed one way or another and you will not be free until he is. Do you want to know something funny?" Emma asked.

Faye ground her teeth together and tried in vain to get up. "No," she spat.

Ignoring her reply, Emma continued, "Your brother came here after he split up from you. We told him about what we hoped to achieve and he told us that you now had the pendant. When he refused to help us, we tried to contain him. It worked for a few hours but then your beloved friend David helped him to escape. Dax said he was going to find you before the resistance did, so naturally we couldn't let that happen. I ordered David and Mat to find you before he did and do whatever was necessary to bring you back here first."

"You witch," Faye spat again. "Where the hell is my brother?"

Emma's face twisted into a smirk. "I wouldn't worry about your brother Faye; I'd say that's the least of your worries. Besides, I hadn't finished talking.

"Your father found out from Dax that we were planning to destroy Fynn through you and immediately set out to find how much time he had left to stop us. But in searching for this, he found out what we already knew about the decision that was going to be made. He changed tact and entered this time into his watch instead. He was on his way to give it to you when we dispatched some members to remove him. On his way home, he ran into Kash and we lost track of the watch. It just so happened that Kash turned up here looking for you and everything sort of fell into place.

"Lark coming here was an added bonus. When you failed to collect the information necessary to complete the Runner transformation, I thought all hope was lost. You saved us when you identified him as a Runner and all we had to do was get him out of the way. All we need is his finger print sample. It's lucky that his prints have been all over this watch.

"Really we should be thanking you Faye. If it weren't for you, none of this would have been possible."

Faye sat in stunned silence. Again, Emma had found a way of making no sense at all. This couldn't be true. You couldn't make someone a Runner by their finger print alone, it was crazy! Just what kind of twisted world had she fallen into? She would not help these maniacs complete a revenge fueled crusade.

"I honestly don't know why you think I'll help you," Faye laughed. "I've never had any real intention to help you. You can't make me."

Emma's eyes went dark and she smiled wryly. "Oh but I can Faye. Let's just say I have methods of gentle persuasion."

She stood up and winked at Faye as she walked toward the basement. "It's nothing personal Anna," she grinned, then disappeared behind the bar.

Chapter 26
The Runner Experience

Twenty minutes passed and Faye was sat in the same position Emma had left her in. Mat stood behind her with his hands on her shoulders and Kash was now similarly detained in case she went to get help.

Kash stared at Faye who looked completely lost in thought and muttered, "I'm so sorry. If I'd have known this would've happened then I never would've come here. Faye, I don't want to see you get hurt." There was something final in the way she said this and Faye tried to get up.

"Just stop struggling Faye, it's easier then," Mat demanded.

Faye glanced at Kash and smiled weakly, then turned her head to glare at her captor. Then she said to him, "Why do you do it? I mean, this isn't the resistance I know. Once you probably had morals and standards, but now? You're just a broken toy soldier; the result of a child throwing a strop to get their own way."

Obviously this cut Mat deep, but he gritted his teeth and continued to stare straight ahead, ignoring Faye's attempts to rile him.

There had to be a way to at least free Kash, if not herself. If only Faye could talk to her then they could come up with a decent plan. Just as Faye tried to think up an escape, she heard the trap door open and Emma walked to the table flanked by two burly looking students.

"I'd ask if you're ready, but you wouldn't get the option to say no anyway," Emma laughed.

The two stocky students headed for Faye and Mat stepped

away from her shoulders.

Before they reached her, Faye said to Emma, "Actually, can I go to the toilet before we start?" Faye shot a quick glance at Kash, then continued, "C'mon, don't you trust me?"

Emma folded her arms. "No, not particularly." There was an undertone of skepticism to her voice but she waved Faye in the direction of the stairs regardless. "Since you're going to become a Runner in a short amount of time anyway, you might as well."

As she began to get up, Kash turned to Emma. "Can I go too? If you're sending guards to wait outside anyway then I might as well."

Now Emma was even more suspicious and eyed the two girls cautiously. Deciding they couldn't escape, she agreed to let them go. All Faye needed was time to talk. Just a minute to talk.

The Inn stairs were steep and Faye passed the room she'd been given on the way. Curious pairs of eyes peeked at them from behind jarred doors as they walked by and the two accompanying students kept ushering the girls to walk quicker.

When they reached the toilet, one of the students demanded, "Be quick, we'll be waiting outside."

"Fine, jeez give us girls some privacy!" Faye joked as she pushed open the old wooden door. As soon as Kash was safely inside, Faye grabbed her arm and pulled her close enough to have a whispered conversation.

"I have a plan," Faye said in a hushed voice. "But it will require precision."

Kash looked at the concentrated girl. "Okay, I'm all ears. I'm up for whatever plan you have that doesn't involve us staying here."

Faye glanced quickly at the door. "After I'm 'transformed', I'll suggest that I go through Mara first to pick up supplies or something. Then when I step into the streetlight, you tell Emma you want to say goodbye and I grab your arm at the last minute. It is vital that you are near enough for me to do this otherwise I can't get you out of here. What do you think?"

Kash was almost speechless. How could she think something up like that so quickly! "I think it's a brilliant plan, but a bit ridiculous," Kash admired, then she flung her arms around Faye and said rather loudly, "Please be okay when you get back from the Runner transforming thing!"

"I'm sure I will be," Faye assured her, then opened the door into the corridor where the students were waiting.

It didn't take them long to get back downstairs and they found Emma waiting for them in the bar. "Kash stays here but Faye comes with me," she announced. Then she turned to address the students. "You stay here with Miss Trix, I'm sure I'll be fine on my own."

Kash was sat back down on one of the wooden chairs and Faye was marched over to her waiting trainer.

"I'm sure we won't have any problems," Emma said sweetly, as she maneuvered Faye in front of her and rammed a gun into the small of her back.

"You don't really leave me much choice do you," Faye snapped, as she was forced down the basement steps to the open barrel.

They wound their way through the twisting tunnel to the room with six doors that Faye had seen before. Emma stopped in the middle of the cave and turned Faye to face her.

Pressing the gun lightly to Faye's forehead and removing the safety catch, Emma asked, "Are you going to help me, or do I have to use persuasion?"

Faye knew she really only had one option. She wasn't prepared to be tortured again, just to end up helping this maniac of a woman anyway.

Grinding her teeth together, Faye replied, "Just tell me what I have to do."

Emma took a few steps forward, making Faye walk backwards with the gun still trained on her head and nodded to someone. Faye heard a click behind her as a door swung open and bright white light spilled out around her.

She was just in time to see Emma smile before someone behind her pressed a cloth over her mouth and dragged her into the empty space.

The door slammed and disappeared at the same time that Emma seemed to vanish. Faye struggled and kicked, trying to break free from this unknown force, but was just met with a much stronger resistance.

The edges of her vision started to blur and she realized it was the same gas they'd used to kidnap her. As this person began to lay her down on the floor, Faye felt a burning sensation in her neck. Before she could make out what was wrong with her neck, her vision finally went black and similar to the previous time, the last

Prisms

thing she saw was Mat's apologetic face.

* * *

As Faye came to, everything felt numb. This sensation didn't last long though and she stretched out the new aches in her body. The numbness was then replaced with a sensation she found hard to describe.

It was kind of like little waves of energy under her skin or a light buzzing. This lasted for a few minutes as Faye regained her sight and noticed she was in a blank, white, square room. No window, no bed, nothing but empty space. Faye stood up slowly and stretched out the tensions in her body, but quickly became aware this was a terrible idea.

As soon as she stood there was a burning, stinging feeling in her neck. This rapidly turned into excruciating pain and had spread round her body in a matter of seconds.

The burning spasmed through her and made her drop to her knees. She twisted and writhed in agony in an attempt to be rid of the shockwaves, but it continued to spread very quickly. Normally Faye had a very high threshold for pain, but this was unlike anything she'd ever experienced.

She curled up in a ball on the floor waiting for the agony to be over and passed out.

* * *

When Faye regained consciousness, everything seemed to be so much brighter. She noticed that she was in exactly the same room, but the pain was gone.

As she went to stand up, she felt stronger than she had done in a long while. There was this indescribable energy that pulsed through her veins and she suddenly had the urge to run. She sprinted across the room and almost hit the other wall. Her speed surprised her, but she wasn't scared by it. In fact, she enjoyed feeling so ... alive.

Testing her new energy and abilities, Faye noticed something in the room was different. A full length mirror now stood propped against the corner and she jogged over to investigate it.

Her reflection looked pretty much the same, apart from her more angular cheek bones and brighter Maran colors. Her eyes were thankfully still the same old color and not the ghostly opal of the men she'd run into in the Lamplight. It was weird that her colors were brighter though. The patch on her neck must've been removed.

She checked this in the mirror and noticed something even odder. Her birthmark now had another line through it and looked raw to touch. Perhaps this was what had caused her so much pain.

As she contemplated this, one of the blank white walls turned into a transparent pane of greyish glass and she saw Emma behind it, sitting among several spaced out chairs and a large fridge. So that's why they call it an observation room, Faye thought.

Emma's voice echoed round the room like a loudspeaker. "How do you feel?"

Faye again stretched out her limbs and replied, "Yeah I feel great. I feel ... rejuvenated. Now let me out and I'll rip your head off."

Emma beamed at her. "Then I think you're ready."

At least this meant Faye could leave the oppressive Inn but as the door reappeared, she questioned, "What exactly is different about me?"

Emma got up and walked over to the pane of glass and stood opposite Faye. "You're virtually invincible. Nothing can stop you from destroying Fynn now."

This was fantastic news. If nothing could stop her, she could go ahead with her own plan. Emma had just made the biggest mistake of her life.

As soon as she entered the Lamplight, Faye would play by her own rules. She could do whatever it took to get her family back and no one was going to stand in her way. Maybe this Runner thing wasn't so bad after all.

Chapter 27
Run Runner Run

After Emma had shown the new honoree Runner out of the empty white room, she'd handed Faye the beeping red timer. Two hours left for her to get inside the Lamplight and stop this decision, whatever it may be.

Faye held back the rising urge to hit Emma.

She was growing accustomed to the damp earthy smell of the winding tunnels and was even beginning to feel safe walking down them. Just as she was about to step through the open barrel, Emma put her arm across the exit and reached into one of her pockets. Wary of what she was doing, Faye took a quick step back so that she was pressed against the cold rock wall. Pulling her hand out again, Emma produced a small black patch. Different in color to the one that let you travel between Earth and Mara but around roughly the same size.

"This," Emma said signaling to the small square in her hand, "will mask your Runner abilities. When wearing it you will not feel any different to your normal Maran self. It is imperative that you only remove it when necessary."

There was something about the way she said this that made Faye uneasy, so she asked, "What happens when I remove it then?"

Emma looked down at her feet and bit the inside of her cheek. "Well, obviously your Runner abilities will return but we don't know what impact it will have on your body. It's probably safe though."

Faye looked incredulously at her trainer. "Probably? You don't even know if it's safe!?" How could Emma not have told her this before!

"I'm sure it's safe, we just don't know how long your body can function with these abilities before it … well … shuts down or something."

Great. She was stuck with these new amazing abilities that just might kill her. "Well that's wonderful Emma," she said scornfully. "Hey, how about you implant a bomb in my stomach to see if it goes off. Or, maybe, you want to attach blow torches to my feet to see if I'll fly!" Faye shouted, torn between being sarcastic and being extremely angry. "Maybe then I might not die!"

In between the sniggering Emma looked genuinely apologetic, but Faye was past waiting for excuses.

"Just give me the damn patch," she demanded.

Emma handed over the black square and cautioned, "Careful, it might sting a bit."

"I really couldn't care less you witch," Faye said, glaring at Emma with the best evils she could muster. She carefully removed the adhesive back and felt for the new mark on her neck. Then placing the patch over it, Faye screamed and cursed as her neck again began to burn. It didn't last as long as the original transformation but it was just as painful.

"That stung like hell you liar!" Faye accused Emma.

In return, Emma grinned and removed the arm that was blocking her exit. Faye glared one last time at the woman and marched toward the basement steps. Inside the bar, she could still see Kash detained by the two stocky students. They were all fixated on the television, all apparently watching the same news story over and over again.

Mat shouted to Faye. "Quick, come and have a look at this!" She rushed over to the small box TV and stood waiting for the story to start.

A news presenter appeared on screen. "Good morning. This breaking news has been released only moments ago by members of the conference. A suspected terrorist has been detained in the quiet town of Hem in the last hour by an elite Runner squad. Lark Lyre is suspected of releasing a nerve gas into both worldly atmospheres and paralyzing the population for a length of five days. It is unclear how he spent his time, or even how he acquired the gas, however we have been informed that the nephew of late world leader Jonathon Caine is a rogue Runner himself. We will continue to follow the story as it unfolds."

Lark's face appeared on screen as a mug shot and Faye went to sit down by Kash. She was quietly sobbing into her hand. "They've got my brother. I'm never going to see Lark again," she murmured.

Faye could relate to how she was feeling. After all, she had no idea where Dax was or even if her father was still alive.

Draping one arm around Kash's shoulder, Faye said quietly, "Kash listen to me, I promise I will find Lark when I'm in the Lamplight. I will make it my first priority to find him, I promise."

Kash nodded and wiped away some of the tears that were rolling down her cheeks.

"Hey, you need to be strong now," Faye reassured her. "You really need to be strong for me and Lark."

Something in Kash's mind registered and she straightened up in her chair. This sudden change in emotion surprised the students and they all reached for their guns, just in case.

Mat waved one of his hands in their direction. "Don't be so stupid. What on Mara do you need a gun for?!" he commanded.

The students looked sheepishly at each other and dropped their arms to their sides.

Mat turned to Faye. "Can I have a word?" Realizing Emma was watching them intently, he added, "In private?"

Faye couldn't think of any reason not to and nodded. "I don't have anything I want to say to you. But hell, why not. I'm probably going to die soon anyway," she joked.

This made Mat uncomfortable but he motioned for her to follow him anyway.

He led her down through the barrel tunnels and helped her collect supplies. Faye took a stinger in case of close encounters, and although she'd never fired one before, she also loaded a gun with six bullets. Mat gave her a quick crash course on how to fire it, but it was going to be very hit and miss with her behind the barrel. It was too risky to carry any extra ammo because it would weigh her pockets down, so she would have to make do with just six. She changed into an all-black stream lined suit and concealed the pendant under her top.

Since she would be going to Centar first, Faye really hoped that

Kash would realize to take off the patch in the light. She'd forgotten to tell her that.

Mat insisted on giving Faye a prep talk, reminding her about who her father really worked for and that her main priority was to find Torre Fynn. Even though she really hated him at the moment, Mat had a knack of calming her nerves. It was in the way his words all blended together and in the way his smile revealed very small but prominent dimples in his cheeks. But then Faye would remember how he had betrayed her and David, and she would hate him again.

Once they reappeared in the bar, Emma rushed over and checked how long was left on the timer. 1 hour and 30 minutes.

"Faye you have to go NOW," Emma ordered, ushering her toward the back door. Since the front streetlight had recently been smashed, Mat told her that she would have to use the one outside the back instead.

Just as Faye reached the door, she turned. "Emma, I'm going to Centar first. If I don't make it out of the Lamplight then I want one last look at my home. There shouldn't be any Runners out patrolling, I'll be quick I promise. Also can Kash come out and say goodbye?"

Faye brushed one hand over her neck as she said this and Kash nodded very subtly as she confirmed, "I really would like to say goodbye to Faye. You know … just in case."

Emma surveyed both the girls warily. "My, my Miss Link, you do ask for a lot."

Faye walked over to her deliberating trainer. "Emma, I'm going to destroy Torre for you. You owe me this much at least," she pleaded.

Emma's face became twisted with revenge and she reluctantly agreed to what Faye was asking. "Seriously Faye, you'd better be damn quick in Centar because you need to get inside the Lamplight."

The two bulky students stepped away from Kash and Mat gestured for her to walk with Faye. When she was just within earshot, Faye whispered, "When we're standing in the light you need to take off the patch when I tell you to and hold onto my arm." This plan had better work, Faye thought.

There was a chill in the air outside and the temperature was noticeably colder than earlier. Early morning mist twisted around the lamppost and hung in thick sheets along the black alley.

Emma pointed for Faye to stand in the light. "Remember, quick in Centar then the Lamplight. Good luck Faye, we're all counting on you. Destroy Fynn."

"No pressure then," Faye muttered back. Emma stepped slowly to one side and let Kash through to say goodbye. The small gathering outside the pub watched carefully as Kash got nearer to the streetlight. Then she flung her arms around Faye, concealing the patch on her neck.

Faye reached for the pendant round her neck, using Kash to shield the motion from the waiting resistance members.

"See you later everyone," Faye addressed to the small crowd.

As soon as she felt Kash reach for her own patch, Faye shouted, "Now, do it!"

Before anyone could react or stop them, Faye and Kash disappeared into the light. There was a mild jolting sensation then both girls were stood outside the Link household. Kash noticed the large iron gates were coated in ice but she was grateful that she was no longer aware of the changing temperature.

Faye pulled out of the hug and spoke urgently. "Kash wait here at our house and I'll find Lark as soon as I can. I'll find Dax as well, once I figure out where he is."

Kash stared at Faye in disbelief. "You really can't be so stupid to think I just wanted to escape?" Faye was now completely confused and listened as she continued, "I want to help in whatever way I can."

This was a relief for Faye but worry also crossed her mind as she considered everything that could possibly go wrong. On one hand she would be grateful for any help she could get, but on the other hand she didn't want to involve anyone else.

A few minutes passed while she weighed up her options. "Fine. I need whatever help I can get. Kash wait here for ten minutes while I run ahead to make sure it's safe. Smash the streetlight first so they can't follow us through. When ten minutes have passed, head for the main square along the street, where you first met Dax and I'll meet you somewhere up there, okay?" It was a pretty thorough plan and it didn't sound like there was any room for negotiation in the details.

"I'll wait here then, but just be careful Faye," Kash warned. "If anything happens to you, I will murder you myself."

This made Faye grin and she squeezed Kash's hand before she raced off into the darkness.

Houses blurred past her as she headed for the main square, racing through the silent suburban streets. It only took her three minutes to reach the shops district and Faye began to slow as she heard her footsteps echo along the cobbled road. Deciding it was safe enough to continue; she picked up the pace and ran.

Frost danced along the blackened windows of Tine Street as Faye felt the wind whip past her flushed face. All seemed quiet and all looked still, but she knew things were not always as they seemed.

Centar appeared to be safe, but the Lamplight could be merciless and not a place Faye cared to visit again. The memory of her last visit was still sore to touch on and stung bitterly if anyone asked, but thankfully, no one was asking.

She knew all her focus was needed if she was to go any way to succeeding so she dropped even lower to the ground as she raced through the night, avoiding the streetlamps.

The shops she passed were barely visible in the low light and many of the names now unfamiliar to her. The shop fronts had been virtually demolished and many were just empty shells and dusty shelves; a stark comparison to before the Runners.

Remembering this made Faye slow ever so slightly. The violence they brought and the destruction they caused had already taken innocent lives. Innocent lives.

Faye stopped, her breath hung in the cold night air as if suspended in front of her.

"The Runners cannot touch you," Faye reassured herself. "You have the same abilities as them and this new race of Runners don't even know you exist."

Of this, she was sure. They knew about David in London, Lark in Hem and Clare caught between both worlds, but as of yet, they did not know her.

This was the first time Faye had allowed herself to gather her surroundings. Knowing the danger of her wasting time and even being in Centar, Faye climbed part way up the stone wall next to her and crawled behind the shop sign above the doorway.

Prisms

As her eyes adjusted to the unfamiliar darkness, she fiddled with the patch on her neck and reminded herself again of why she was here. But as she tried to find the reminder of why she'd 'joined' the resistance in the first place, she was distracted by the patterns of the street cobbles and rusting blue chair outside 'Simms and Sons' opposite.

She knew this place, and not only did she know it, she remembered twirling a lock of topaz hair between her fingers and swinging her legs on the cobalt chair. Faye grew up in this very street and had once run up and down the silver cobbles for very different reasons to the ones she was forced to run for now.

"Don't let yourself get too involved," Mat had cautioned her in their prep talk. "You get in, you get out. If he's there, your father, he's not the same man he once was. He works for the resistance and if anyone threatens his life or yours, you must reply that he's a stranger to you. Otherwise both of your safety will be compromised."

Faye had tried to heed Mat's word of warning, but it was so hard to see him in that way now and she refused to believe what Mat had told her. It was impossible to trust any member of the resistance.

The silence was broken by screaming from just up the street. Faye's gaze snapped to her right, just in time to see a flash of light that ended the tortured noise. She really hoped that Kash hadn't decided to follow her before ten minutes had passed.

The air again turned still. This was wrong. Faye understood that silence often meant danger and there was no need for the Runners to be out tonight. No one could outrun the Runners. Well, no one but her.

Faye knew at this point she had three options. She could face them and lose the opportunity to reach the Lamplight, or disappear. Normally Faye would just disappear, but not tonight. Tonight was different and she would have to reach Fynn no matter what.

One brief moment of pain and Faye's plan may even succeed. Emma had warned her against it, but right now Faye really didn't care. Choosing the third option and repeating in her mind, "It's just a plaster, it's JUST a plaster," Faye reached for the patch on her neck.

In one swift movement the patch was gone, to be replaced by

Faye's own screaming. Pain spasmed through her, her eyes flaming red as the torture continued.

Waiting for the pain to stop and sensing the Runners gaining speed, Faye finally felt herself changing. The adrenaline kicked up from her legs with such force she was thrown to the ground below. And so, she began her race to find Fynn, before the Runners found her.

Chapter 28
The Reality of War

All of Faye's senses were alive. The throbbing of her pulse had been amplified to allow more blood to flow round her body, giving extra energy to every organ. Already bright Maran colors were illuminated and Faye could smell steak cooking in someone's house miles away. It was an amazing experience but she needed to remember that her priority was to get into the Lamplight.

The streetlamps along this particular road had all been smashed to pieces. Not one remained lit and Faye's only hope was to try the main square. She just hoped she'd be able to find a working light there.

Shops continued to blur past as she sprinted through the quiet street. She heard footsteps a few meters behind her, getting nearer and nearer with each stride. It had to be a Runner because no one else would be able to keep pace with her.

The main square began to come into vision and Faye saw a lamppost, lit and working at the far end. Not far to go, Faye assured herself, and all the while the thud, thud, thud of someone's feet grew louder.

Her head was spinning and pulsating with the adrenaline, every nerve in her body felt electric. Her breath came in short rasps, spilling out into the cold air as the square grew even closer.

Just as she began to near the end of the street a dark figure appeared in the gap, blocking her path. The silhouette didn't move for a while then it began to head toward her. She couldn't stop running in fear of being caught but she couldn't continue to race toward the advancing figure either. Deciding she'd exhausted all her options, she continued toward the silhouette regardless. In the low light she could just about make out the figure of a man; a man in his early twenties perhaps?

The gap between them continued to close rapidly and there were no side alleys for Faye to turn down. Caught in between two fates, but which one should she choose? Time was ticking and there were only a matter of meters left until she'd find out.

Faye began to give up hope and pulled out her gun. The silhouette in front of her faltered momentarily then sped up and became even more urgent to reach her. She removed the safety catch just as the silhouette shouted, "Faye, it's me, don't shoot!"

No, it was impossible! Was it really him? Faye stopped and stood completely still. Her hands were shaking and the cold sweat matted her hair. Every instinct told her to pull the trigger, it was some kind of trick, but it really did sound like him. The man was almost upon her and the footsteps from behind were deafening now.

She had a split second to react or decide what to do, so she lightly lowered the gun. As she did so, the man shouted, "Faye, duck!"

She dropped to the ground and looked up to see two men collide. There was a blinding flash of light and Faye saw the whites of Dax's eyes dim as he disappeared with it. Then silence.

No screaming. No pain. Nothing you'd expect to feel when you lose a loved one. No emotion. Nothing. Just the sound of her own breath.

Faye had just sealed the fate of her brother.

The shock began to slowly dissipate and was replaced with anger. She'd searched for him for so long and had been through hell and back to find him, but now? This monster had removed her brother. This monster had destroyed the last shred of hope that she had in this world. Tears stung Faye's eyes and she ground her teeth as she began to turn and face the attacker.

Still crouched on the ground, Faye stood and slowly swiveled to face them. Why hadn't the Runner tried to remove her?

The dark concealed the identity of the man who had removed her brother, so she reached into one of her pockets and found a lighter that Mat had given her.

Faye flicked the flame into life and the lighter cast shadows across his face. His fringe had fallen over one eye and it seemed that he himself was in shock. His face was a picture of emotion, half surprised, half upset. The true betrayer of her and her family; Lark Lyre.

"You traitor," she spat. "You back stabbing, violent, twisted traitor."

Lark had no reply but just stood in shock.

Faye raised the gun and screamed as she fired the first bullet. Lark reeled back and fell to the ground. He clutched his stomach and tried to speak but the wind had been completely taken out of him.

One of his hands steadied himself as he tried to sit back up and his other hand felt for where the wound should have been.

Confusion played across his face as he tried to find some trace of the bullet. He found not one scar, as if it hadn't even entered his body.

Faye's temper began to boil and she fired the gun four more times shouting, "WHY ... WON'T ... YOU ... DIE!" Each time the bullets just bounced off Lark's skin, having no impact whatsoever.

The Runner now lay in a ball, trying to shield himself from the raining bullets. As Faye ran her hands through her hair and felt the tears begin to flow down her cheeks, she crumpled to the floor and wrapped her hands around her knees, hugging them close to her chest.

Faye heard another set of footsteps getting nearer, so pulled out the stinger and crawled over to where Lark was lying on the ground. It may be her last chance to see him before she was taken away.

"This," she said menacingly as she brandished the stinger by his neck, "is for Dax." Then she thrust the metal rod into his Runner mark and held it there as he writhed and screamed in pain.

Faye felt a pair of arms dragging her away across the cobbles, far from the man crying in agony, which threw her onto her front and pinned both arms behind her. Someone's knee was in the small of her back and Faye struggled against this unknown force. She knew she would probably be stronger than them, but she just didn't have the energy to fight back.

"Faye, calm down," Kash ordered. Her voice was shaky but firm and she refused to lessen her grip.

Faye continued to choke back her tears and cried, "He killed my brother. Dax is gone. Lark killed my brother!" Faye again tried to get up but Kash had found her pressure point.

"Faye listen to me! What happened?!" Kash shouted over the screaming.

Lark half dragged himself over to where Faye was face down on the cobbles and sobbed. "I thought he was a Runner. I thought he was going to kill you, I had to stop him. I'm so sorry, I had no idea … I … I don't know how …" He faltered.

Faye felt her arms loosen slightly as Kash turned to her brother. "Lark … what have you done…?"

The Runner was now fighting back his own tears, stuttering. "Dax … he shouldn't have been here … I … I … I don't understand … it wasn't … if I've removed …" He couldn't even finish his sentence before Kash herself began to shake her head and grind her teeth.

"You … removed … Dax?" she asked furiously. "YOU … removed … my … Fiancé?"

Lark slowly stood up and began to back away from his sister. Her eyes were burning with anger and she was physically shaking as she moved away from Faye and took a few steps toward her brother.

Faye saw her opportunity and lunged at Lark with the stinger.

He jumped back and wailed, "I'm so sorry." He sprinted into the darkness away from the square.

How was Lark out here when the news said he'd been caught? The only explanation was that he wasn't rogue at all. Faye looked at her timer and saw fifty minutes remaining.

"Kash go after him, I'll take care of Fynn and the rest of his foot soldiers," Faye hissed. She was trying so hard to keep a lid on her emotions but she felt her control slipping.

Kash's eyes were focused on the spot where Lark had been and Faye thrust the stinger into her palm. "Use this if you have to, it will work on any Runner you see. I'll find you after I get back and then we'll destroy the resistance. Together."

Kash said nothing but turned to look at Faye with tortured eyes. There was real pain in her face and her calm temper had been shattered. Her fingers formed a tight fist around the stinger and she raced into the darkness after Lark.

Prisms

This was the first time that Faye had been truly alone in a while. Her brother had been removed by her future brother-in-law, her father was probably dead and she didn't even know if her mother was safe. What a messed up family.

Rage bubbled inside of her and Faye picked up the gun she'd dropped. She placed it back into the waistband of her trousers and twisted to look at the square. The streetlight was still on and the path clear for her to access it.

Faye now had her own desire for revenge and she would exact it on the one man who had caused all this violence. The only real way to win would be to fight fire with fire.

Everyone knows there is no wrath like a woman's wrath and Faye would hunt Torre Fynn to the ends of the worlds if she had to.

Time was running out and Fynn would be dead before it did.

Chapter 29
The 300th Floor

Small specks of rain began to fall, changing into sleet as they hit the frosty air. Faye charged along the cobbles toward the main square and checked the timer again. Forty minutes left.

The once thriving square was now a mess of up-turned benches and shattered windows. All merchandise from the shops had either been looted or destroyed and thick frost had managed to creep up one of the shop steps to settle on the wooden ledge by the door. What a difference five days make.

The solitary streetlamp stood by what used to be a bank. Credit cards littered the entrance and hundreds of receipts swirled around, caught in miniature twisters.

This was it. Once inside the Lamplight, Faye couldn't leave until she'd stopped the decision. She couldn't rest until she'd killed Torre Fynn and avenged the many deaths that lay at his hands.

Screw Emma, this was for Faye now.

She centered herself in the orange spotlight and took several deep breaths, watching them hit the wall of ice and frost. The pendant felt heavy in her hands. When inside, she would find David and anyone else imprisoned in the complex.

Faye took one last look at the destruction around her and twisted the pendant between her fingers. This time something very odd happened. The prism seemed to float in the air in front of her, suspended by some invisible force. It continued to twist, spinning faster and faster until there was a blinding flash of white light. Faye stood perfectly still, undisturbed by any jolt or transition between the places. When she looked round for a second time, polished black towers loomed over head and spanned for miles in every direction.

The main complex was directly ahead of Faye, but she felt a nagging at the back of her mind that again told her something wasn't right. Not one Runner patrolled the grounds, not one guard appeared in the exit. It was as if the place were deserted. At least this would make it easier for Faye to find Fynn.

She sprinted to the only entrance of the main tower and looked up at the building that seemed to stretch forever into the sky. The shiny double doors were wide open and through them, Faye couldn't see anyone inside.

Walking into the reception area, Faye noticed it was a blank white room with a single black desk. Several screens cluttered the walls and one lift sat in the corner.

Faye presumed this was the only way to access the different floors of the tower, but now she was inside the Lamplight, she didn't really know what to do. How could she possibly know where this decision was going to take place?

The logical thing to do was to get in the lift and take it from there. Again, Faye seemed to be having a great deal of luck and was able to stroll through the doors without so much as a Runner in sight.

One of the panels inside the lift sported a logo that matched the new mark on her neck, while another boasted 300 buttons, each labeled differently. With thirty minutes remaining on the timer, it would be impossible to check every floor. Pressing them at random wouldn't get Faye any further either.

She quickly scanned the many floors and noticed that from 280-300, they were not labeled. However, she did come across one floor marked 'detention'. Perhaps this was where she could find David.

After Faye pressed the 121st floor button to 'detention', the doors slammed shut and the lift shot upwards. The sheer speed made Faye temporarily loose her balance and she remained in a heap on the floor until the lift had stopped. It just seemed safer that way.

The doors opened to reveal a matte black reception, very similar to the one on the first floor but with more technology. The main desk was a low cube in the middle of a vast room, with numerous doors around it. Each door had an individual pane of grey glass on the front with a name on the wall next to it.

Time was rapidly running out but finding one of the detainees might be her only hope. She began to run a circuit around the desk, watching as names blurred past her. Sam Owens, Jemma Torne, Becca Strider, Rakel Vey, numerous names that she didn't recognize.

As she continued to run, one name made her stop abruptly. Clare Fynn. Hadn't Clare also been accused of terrorism on the news? If she was the daughter of Torre Fynn, she might be able to help.

Faye tried to stare through the grey glass but it was virtually impossible to see past. There had to be some way of opening the door.

Inspecting the grey panel again, Faye noticed the outline of a hand indented into it. Maybe it was like a finger print reader.

She rolled up one of her sleeves slightly and pressed her palm against the screen. A quiet whirring noise drifted from the door then an automated voice said, "Runner". The door slid up and Faye could see a square white room, however it didn't appear to have anyone in it.

There was a bed that looked like it had been slept in and a cube in the corner, but where was Clare?

Faye took one step into the room and gasped as she was hit with a metal chair.

"What the hell?" she shouted, trying to pick herself up off the floor whilst rubbing her head at the same time. Faye grabbed one of the metal legs and threw the chair behind her. It smashed into the black desk and clattered onto the floor. Then Faye swung the attacker out of the room and pinned them by the neck with her arm. The attacker struggled for a bit, then stopped and laughed in surprise.

Faye could feel herself becoming more agitated and pressed harder against their neck. This only made them laugh more and they tilted their head so Faye could see their neck. It bore a mark very similar to how Faye's used to be before the transformation.

"Faye, I'm so sorry," Clare giggled. "Look can you please put me down now, because it's kind of starting to hurt."

Now speechless, Faye removed her arm and caught Clare before she fell. "I thought you were a Runner," Clare admitted. This was very surreal. The person who had just hit her with a chair was a teenage girl. Her picture on the news had made her seem much older.

Faye looked in confusion at Clare. "Why did you hit me with a chair?"

Clare laughed again. "I've told you, I thought you were a Runner that had been left behind."

Faye picked up on the last part of the sentence and questioned her. "What do you mean 'left behind'?"

Now it was Clare's turn to be confused. "So, you don't work for the conference?" she asked.

One of Faye's hands clenched into a fist and she shouted, "No! Do I look like I work for the conference?!"

Clare smirked then Faye calmed herself momentarily and continued, "Where have all the Runners gone, Clare?"

Clare bit her lip, as if deciding as to whether she should share her information or not. "I don't know where they've gone, but an announcement to evacuate the towers was played over the speakers about one hour ago. My fath ... Torre Fynn," she corrected herself, "came in here and said he'd collect me after he'd sorted out something. Something about a decision?"

Faye grabbed the tops of Clare's arms and spoke urgently. "Wait, wait, wait. Fynn's the one who makes the decision? Where is he?"

Clare was taken aback by Faye's sudden urgency and waited a moment before she answered. "I don't know if he's the one who makes the decision," she emphasized sarcastically, "but he's probably in his office."

Faye heard the timer beep and noticed she had ten minutes remaining. How could twenty minutes already have passed!

"Clare, where is Fynn's office?" Faye demanded. She could feel the adrenaline beginning to course round her body again and her Runner abilities strengthening. Some natural instinct had kicked in. Perhaps it was the most basic instinct of all; to survive.

Clare looked into Faye's eyes and saw a mixture of anger and desperation. "It's the top most floor, you can't get any higher without going on the roof. The 300th floor."

Faye leant forward and squeezed Clare's shoulder as she said, "Thank you." But just before she turned to leave, Faye remembered.

"Oh Clare, can you do me a favor? Check these cells for a David Pringle. When you find him, try and use the computers or something to release him. I'll find both of you afterwards but promise me you'll get out of the Lamplight as soon as you do."

"After what?" Clare asked puzzled. "Just promise!" Faye shouted, panic rising in her voice. Clare nodded once. "As soon as I find this David person."

Faye smiled and raced back to the lift. She watched as the doors slammed and the 300th floor button began to flash. It was unlikely Clare would be able to free him, but if she was anywhere near as resourceful as Torre, she shouldn't have a problem. Faye braced herself, but still crumpled to the floor as the lift continued to climb.

297, 98, 99, 300. The 300th floor; Faye should've guessed. The doors slid open and in the room behind a large marble desk, stood Torre Fynn. One hand poised above a hole in the desk with a metal rod and the other clasping a gun.

The only question was; who could pull the trigger first?

Chapter 30
The Clock Tolls

Faye flicked the gun up and removed the safety catch all in one fluid motion. Fynn's face was a picture of confusion and he raised his gun a split second after her.

It was crucial Faye didn't miss. She'd already wasted five bullets and she had one bullet left. If the next shot she fired didn't hit Torre, she'd have no hope of succeeding.

Her finger twitched on the trigger as beads of sweat began to form across her forehead and she heard the bullet leave the gun.

She flew forward and watched as her gun skidded across to where Torre stood. One of his feet stopped it from sliding further, while the other lightly kicked his chair out of the way.

Faye didn't understand. Fynn hadn't fired but neither had she, so where had the bullet come from? She collapsed onto the floor and felt a stab of pain between her shoulder blades. The bullet she'd heard hadn't been hers.

She felt someone else's barrel press into the small of her back, forcing her onto her feet. Faye had no idea who this person was but they were dangerous and spontaneous, a lethal combination.

Fynn smiled and laughed. "The one fatal flaw in a Runner's design? An exposed weak point in the dip of their back. I must admit though Faye, I am the tiniest bit curious as to how you acquired these Runner abilities."

The adrenaline still coursed through her body but her brain told her not to move a muscle. Instead, she gritted her teeth and stared at a visible hole in Fynn's desk.

Fynn noticed and followed her gaze, then remarked, "Ingenious, really. I didn't actually design the Lamplight but with any design, again, there is always a flaw."

Faye could feel herself beginning to lose control. She shifted nervously on the spot, fighting the urge to move in case the cold metal against her back became the bullet in her back. "Where have all the Runners gone?"

She heard someone cock the gun behind her and Fynn tutted. "Anna, Anna, Anna. You are in no position to be making any inquiries or demands. I could crush you right now."

His voice had an edge to it that made Faye extremely uneasy. The tone was too calm to match its intent.

"However, as your little sabotage attempt is of no consequence to my plans, I suppose I could probably tell you. The final speech as the 'bad guy' reveals all to the hopeless hero. I love this part."

The timer beeped three times and Faye noticed the digits flash '5 minutes'.

Fynn glared at the watch and marched over to snatch it from Faye.

"What is this, some kind of bomb?" Fynn shouted. Faye grinned and began to laugh. This only made Fynn more agitated and as she continued to laugh, he drew his arm back and hit her across the face with the back of his hand.

It made her cheek smart and the laughing stopped abruptly. A small red mark began to appear, while small pockets of salty tears welled in Faye's eyes.

All niceties, if there had ever been any, were now gone. The air was full of tension and Fynn was very much in control of the situation.

"I will not be mocked by a little, unruly girl!" Fynn hollered. "This exact lack of order is what has forced me to bring about this change."

Faye had so many sarcastic responses lined up in her head, but bit her tongue to stop herself from saying anything else she might regret.

"Well? Ask me what I'm talking about!" Fynn boomed, flecks of spit landing on Faye's face as he shouted into it.

"What change?" Faye whispered, trying to mentally gauge the reaction speed of her restrainer. Fynn walked back to his desk and picked up the metal rod he'd put there only moments ago. He weighed it in his hands then thrust it in front of Faye.

"This is the object that could have saved every insignificant life on Earth and Mara." Fynn indicated to the rod. "On recent reflection, however, it has come to my attention that the world's population just cannot be controlled. Citizens from each world influence those from the other and it is because of the Lamplight that order cannot be maintained.

"There is too much crime, too many illegal passings and all because of communication between the two worlds. It's clear to me now that the worlds are wild, lawless wastelands. They're flawed without a fix."

Faye tried to piece together everything the estranged man was saying, but could find no fit.

Fynn continued. "The only solution? Remove the cause and order will follow. Order will always follow."

If Faye was beginning to understand correctly, then what Fynn proposed to do was madness.

"I therefore have come to the decision that the only possible solution is to collapse the Lamplight."

This was it. The decision Faye had apparently been destined to stop and she couldn't see any way to halt it. If the Lamplight did collapse, then how would that affect the careful balance between the two worlds? If a gap between them had been created to house the Lamplight, then what would happen when it was removed again?

"Fynn, that's insane. If you collapse the Lamplight, then ..." Faye stopped, distracted by the faltering resolve of her restrainer as the metal twitched at her back. Fynn's eyes were a picture of menace. It was painted across his face and stitched into every inch of his being.

"Oh, I know perfectly well what could happen." Fynn grinned. "But at this stage, it seems the only solution. Obliterate the corruption and destruction to replace it with an endless peace."

"Fynn, not only are you now completely mad but you're also being annoyingly cryptic," Faye accused the leader. She didn't want to push the man too much though. It looked to her like he was balancing on the very tip of a mountain and any opposition might just push him right over the edge.

"If I were to collapse the Lamplight ..." Fynn mused, building the suspense. "Then the two worlds might collide. At the point of impact, both would be instantaneously destroyed. Boom." He grinned.

Faye couldn't even begin to understand the true extent of this chaos. It was far beyond insanity and Fynn was willing to mass murder billions upon billions of people to achieve an eternal order for himself.

"You sadistic ... twisted ... man," Faye hissed.

Fynn's eyes were again full of fury. "Don't test me girl."

The worlds colliding. This was what Faye had to stop and all because she was apparently the only one who could use this mysterious pendant. No, it wouldn't happen. More twitching behind her. Just another minute and Faye could spin faster than the trigger could move.

She reached up and carefully pulled the prism from round her neck, trying to make no sudden movements. It seemed stupid that such a small pendant was so important.

Fynn watched as she did this and Faye saw his eyes alight with excitement. He stopped his furious pacing and strode back to Faye. Prizing her hand open, he stood in awe and gazed at the small prism. It was as if nothing else in the world mattered to him more at this moment.

"I didn't think things would work out like this," Fynn admitted. "I knew you had it and I tried to find you, but I never dreamed that you would bring it to me of your own accord."

Faye was now completely lost, but she realized that she may just have made the biggest mistake of her life.

Fynn dropped the metal rod to the floor and snatched the pendant from Faye. They both watched as it hung in the air for a few seconds, splitting each individual color of the spectrum, then Fynn regained his previous urgency.

"Faye, this isn't just some object that lets you travel through the Lamplight," Fynn announced. "This is a key that will allow me to close the Lamplight. Remember I told you everything has a weakness? The one flaw in its design ... is this pendant."

Faye's eyes flashed to the hole in the desk, then to the rod on the floor. Then her brain caught up and realized the enormity of what she'd done. Fynn was going to jam the rod into this switch thing to collapse the Lamplight. Chances are it wouldn't have worked, but then Faye had turned up to offer him the key. She might as well have brought along a silver platter to put it on.

If she was right, then the moment Fynn placed the pendant into the desk, he'd have the power to permanently close the Lamplight.

"No Fynn, you're insane. You'll kill EVERYONE. There will be not one survivor, not even you. You'll make the ultimate sacrifice, but for what? Not life, nor love, nor family but for greed and spite. To spite the worlds that refused to obey your command."

Fynn marched over to his desk and stood with his hand poised above the hole once more. The pendant hung suspended over it and Faye was running out of time. She heard the watch beep and saw on the desk there were two minutes remaining.

"What is it with this stupid watch!" Fynn boomed.

Do or die. Those seemed to be her only two options and if she was going to die anyway, then she might as well try to stop the maniac. A hand clamped round the top of her arm and began to pull Faye backwards.

She had so many unanswered questions. Where was her father? Had Clare managed to free David? If Kash had caught up to Lark, what had happened between them? Had Emma tried to follow when she had disappeared? Why did Dax give her the stupid pendant in the first place!

Faye made up her mind and tensed every muscle in her body. A ticking watch was working against her and the outcome didn't look good as it stood at the moment.

"Fynn don't you dare drop that!" Faye ordered.

Fynn just grinned and let a little chain slip through his fingers.

With her Runner abilities in overdrive, Faye span round and twisted the clamped hand off her arm. The restrainer shrieked with surprise and attempted to adjust their position to combat Faye's attack; but Faye was faster. Kicking out, Faye knocked the gun to the floor and ducked to avoid a flying fist, before grabbing the weapon and ramming the barrel under her opponent's chin. Then she froze.

She couldn't do it. She couldn't react, fire the gun, laugh, cry or move. Every way she looked at the situation, it seemed this scenario was impossible. Faye lowered the gun slightly and found herself fighting back her emotions. She heard Fynn laugh from across the room; the sound bouncing off the polished walls.

"Mum?" she asked. It wasn't really a question. Faye knew who it was; she just couldn't quite believe it.

"Anna," her mother replied. She wore a Runner uniform and now had opal eyes framed by pronounced facial features.

"But you're human, you're not involved! You're normal!" Faye cried, trying desperately to make sense of the situation whilst time ticked on. Her hand wavered and the gun shook ferociously.

Torre shook off his laugh and said, "Surely you knew, Anna?"

Tears left tracks down the side of Faye's face, as she tried to find anything to say. Any words, any sentence. But nothing would come.

"Oh fine, I'll make this really quick. It can be like a little game! Elizabeth and I are brother and sister; you must have known that," Fynn teased, an incredulous expression across his face. "Anyone with intellect has the capacity to find out who their family is, quite easily."

All she needed was one word, but her jaw wouldn't work. Her throat swallowed the sound and let it sink to the pit of her stomach.

"So technically," he continued, "that makes me your uncle. We both thought it best not to tell you, but when the Lamplight was designed, I gave the key to Elizabeth for safe keeping and she passed it to Dax, who then gave it to you.

"She managed to convince Dax that the prism was a gift from your father and would offer help, if you ever needed it. The reality, however, is far more delicious. If you ever tried to use it, it would be more than simple to detain you. Even though I wasn't the sole worldly leader, I had the majority of control. When I removed Jonathon Caine I wanted the key myself, but we completely lost track of you ... yet here you are."

If Faye wasn't so worried about her imminent death, she probably would have been shocked by this revelation. The sound kicked up like fire from her stomach and she shouted, "Why won't people just explain things in simple terms! Why does everyone suddenly seem to be related all of a sudden! Mum, this isn't you. This whole place isn't you. How do you fit into any of it!"

Fynn had been completely in control of her life from the moment she'd been born. The thought made her sick.

"Anna," her mum said. "You can shoot me if you like. It won't change anything."

Faye stood, hands shaking as she tried to find the will to shoot her mother. But as the timer beeped one minute, Faye knew she couldn't.

Elizabeth grinned and leant forward to take the gun back. "I knew you wouldn't shoot me. When this is over darling, I will explain whatever you want to know." Faye aimed the gun several times but couldn't bring herself to pull the trigger. Even if her mum was a Runner and couldn't be killed, she still couldn't shoot her. It just seemed wrong.

Fynn laughed then suddenly gasped as the lift doors opened. Elizabeth twisted round to react, but it wasn't fast enough. Three bullets pelted into her stomach, winding her and rendering her useless. She knocked backwards into Faye before collapsing on the floor. Faye steadied herself to the side and forced herself upright.

David's eyes were wild and Clare stood slightly behind him with another smaller pistol.

Then David ordered, "Faye, stop Fynn!" It was absolutely heartbreaking to see her mother lying on the floor in agony, but Faye remembered that this woman had in fact shot her earlier. Too much to think about now. Too many cogs whirring and sparking in her brain. To hell with being normal, this was far beyond any bounds of normality now.

Faye spun again to face Fynn and ran toward him at a pace that surprised even her. Fynn moved quickly to the desk and held the prism over the gap, but his sluggish reaction speed was no match for Faye's.

Then with the gun only inches from him, Faye shouted, "Fynn drop the pendant away from the desk. I have no problem in firing this gun at you and as far as I'm aware, you're still very much human."

Fynn clasped his hand tighter around the pendant and stared in alarm at the girl now brandishing a weapon.

"Faye," Fynn started, while the timer began to count down from ten seconds. "Dax isn't dead. I know how you can get him back."

Faye faltered, her finger releasing the trigger ever so slightly. "You're lying!" she accused. Fynn dangled the pendant over the desk again and smiled at the inevitability of the outcome.

"If you kill me now, you'll never find him."

Three seconds on the timer.

"Faye, kill him!" someone screamed. A bullet whipped past her hair and shattered the back window of the office. There was a scuffle behind her and more gunfire.

Two seconds on the timer.

"How can I find Dax? Tell me!" Faye shouted. Do or die; her two options.

"Faye, do it now! FAYE!"

"How do I find him!" she hollered again.

One second on the timer.

As Faye began to pull the trigger, several bodies flew past her, all entangled in some way.

Flashes from a gun.

Screaming.

Two figures fall from the window, caught in battle.

Then nothing.

Chapter 31
Prisms

Faye stopped. The air turned silent as she heard pieces of shattered glass sweep across the marbled floor. She opened her hand to feel the pendant caught between her fingers and turned to see the destruction.

She was alone. Stood in a blank white room with white washed walls and a desk with a prism shaped hole in it. There was no window, no destruction, no David, nothing. Just endless nothing.

A screen appeared across the length of a wall that replayed the last ten seconds of chaos. Faye holding the gun, Faye firing the gun, David running at her, Torre falling, Clare screaming. It was all there on the screen. Her life on a wall in front of her. Except that she wasn't in it. She just watched from the outside.

A door appeared in one of the walls and Dax walked through. Faye dropped to her knees as the screen flicked off. The prism clattered to the floor and Faye's face turned dark.

"Welcome to the flipside," Dax said.

The End.

About the Author

Photo © Doug Hart

Amy Durrant is a Journalism student at the University of Sheffield, UK. Amy is also the founder and editor of the music webzine We Are Unseen (www.weareunseen.co.uk). She has had work published for NME, Kerrang!, The Daily Express and on pocket-lint.com, alongside having designed a game for the original iPod Nano. In her spare time she writes poetry, songs and enjoys idling away days in the sunshine with her guitar.

www.amydurrant.com

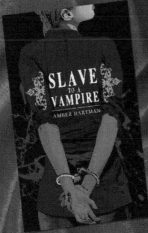

SLAVE
TO A
VAMPIRE

AMBER HARTMAN

Small town girl, Anya, leaves her home in hopes of finding love and adventure after a life filled with lies and masquerades. Waiting to embark on her adventure, she finds herself alone in a park with a bush calling her name. Curiosity killed the cat, as they say, and Anya gets kidnapped and traded to a mysterious man with a secret. Dacio, a charming but dangerous vampire, suddenly finds himself the new owner of the irresistible girl but soon faces a dilemma: should he allow himself to love the feisty young woman, or forcibly keep her at arm's length for her own good? With a whirlwind of broken bones, tears and quick witted humor, the two realize their magnetic but hazardous love cannot be ignored, and with the past behind them they try to fight what they are in hopes of what they can become. With danger awaiting them around every corner, will they answer life's biggest question: Can love truly conquer all, or are they doomed to end in tragedy? With Anya, a slave to a vampire, and Dacio, a slave to his own love, who shall emerge unscathed?

Price: $14.95
ISBN: 978-1-937758-08-0
Library of Congress Control Number: 2012932947

Rainstorm Press   WWW.RAINSTORMPRESS.COM
BOOKS TO READ ON A RAINY DAY

nobody wakes up pretty
diane lefer

New York City, 1992. For Holly,
it's the summer when the city
she's lived in all her life
changes past recognition. And
the funerals are about to
begin.
"Let's get this out of the
way," she says. "I'm a white
woman who likes black men." That
includes her lover Samps. Once a young artist of
promise, he's now homeless, living in a Harlem squat,
and maybe, Holly fears, clinically insane.
But that doesn't explain why she's caught up in a web that
connects Jewish, Italian, and black organized crime. Or
what any of this has to do with the midtown law firm where
she temps, a missing Haitian girl, and a world-famous
Japanese monkey.
Her friends are getting shot. She and Samps can try to
save themselves--or do what they can to stop the killing.

Price: $12.95
ISBN 13 978-1-937758-12-7

Rainstorm
Press
www.RAINSTORMPRESS.COM
BOOKS TO READ ON A RAINY DAY

A DISCRIMINATING DEATH

a novel by

SUSAN DORSEY

The future is looking bright for Jane, a hairdresser in Knoxville, Tennessee. She and her best friend Rodney are opening a new salon in a few short weeks. Their plans begin to unravel when a favorite client suddenly disappears after giving a genealogy lecture about the Melungeons. According to legend, this mysterious group of dark-skinned people had already settled in East Tennessee before the English arrived in the late 1700's.

Although history has hidden the facts about the Melungeons, Jane knows that the key to finding a killer lies buried somewhere in their past. She must discover the truth if she is going to have any future at all.

Price: $14.95
ISBN 13 – 978-1-937758-16-5
Library of Congress Control Number: 2012937221

Rainstorm Press **WWW.RAINSTORMPRESS.COM**
BOOKS TO READ ON A RAINY DAY